FIRED
CAGED

MAYA CHHABRA

Firebird Caged © 2025 by North Star Editions, Mendota Heights, MN 55120. All rights reserved. No part of this book may be used or reproduced in any manner whatsoever, including internet usage, without written permission from the copyright owner, except in the case of brief quotations embodied in critical articles and reviews.

Book design by Karli Kruse
Cover design by Karli Kruse
Cover and title page photographs by Shutterstock Images

Published in the United States by Jolly Fish Press, an imprint of North Star Editions, Inc.

This is a work of fiction. Names, characters, places, and incidents are either the product of the author's imagination or are used fictitiously, and any resemblance to actual persons living or dead, business establishments, events, or locales is entirely coincidental.

Library of Congress Cataloging-in-Publication Data (pending)
978-1-63163-837-4 (paperback)
978-1-63163-836-7 (hardcover)

Jolly Fish Press
North Star Editions, Inc.
2297 Waters Drive
Mendota Heights, MN 55120
www.jollyfishpress.com

Printed in the United States of America

FIREBIRD CAGED

MAYA CHHABRA

JOLLY FISH PRESS
Mendota Heights, Minnesota

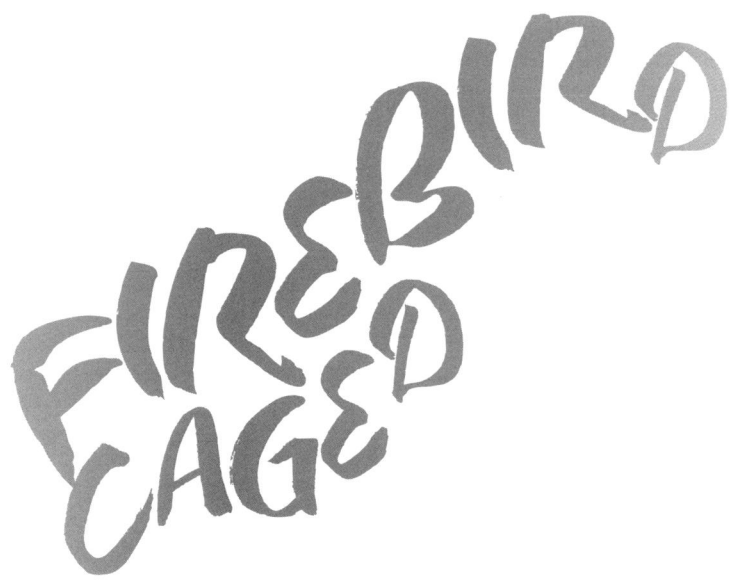

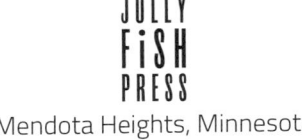

CHAPTER 1

The pregnancy test is hiding in my backpack. The one I picked up from CVS before school. In three hours, I'll be home. I'll know my fate.

But right now, it's still lunch break. And Danny's still talking to Jasleen. I wish he would go away. He knows it's awkward. He shoots me a glance. *Sorry*, he says without words. But Jasleen goes on about *Disco Elysium*. And Danny stays.

Danny and I started dating in July. All summer, I hung around the ice cream shop where he works. After school started, we got serious. I'd never felt like that before, melting at the thought of a guy. Then the shine wore off. We broke up a month ago. He skipped my dance group's performance for some stupid Twitch stream. This was *after* he told me he'd come. It wasn't a big deal, but it was. We had a huge blowout fight, and then—it was over.

Next to me, Madi glares daggers at him. At Jasleen, who's supposed to be my friend too. Who's in my same YWCA dance group. But she'd rather talk video games than send him off. I don't care. I'm not bitter. They can talk. I wouldn't mind so much on any other day.

It's just . . . the pregnancy test in my backpack. It feels like it should set off alarms beeping everywhere. Like it's radioactive.

My last period never came. It's two weeks late now.

The box sits on top of my textbooks. For something that could change everything, the test doesn't weigh much. It's small. But one corner of the box pushes out the worn fabric of the backpack. Somehow, I'm afraid Danny will just know.

It's probably nothing. Maybe I'm sick. Or stressed. Stress can mess with your cycle. But the condom broke that last time. So I have to take the test. Still . . . it's nothing. That's what I tell myself.

Danny finally moves away from our table. Jasleen goes back to chewing her grilled cheese like nothing happened.

I don't want them to stop being friends because of me. They've known each other way longer. It just stings. I wish she realized how hard it is right now. But I'm not going to say anything.

Madi huffs. "Would you mind? They *just* broke up last month."

Jasleen looks guilty. "He came up to me. We're friends. I can't ignore him."

"Sorry, I thought you'd put Ashley first—"

"Madi." I can't stand the tension. I nudge her gently with my elbow. "It's okay. Stop."

She looks at me. And then, because she's my best friend, she drops it.

We spend the rest of lunch alone together. Jasleen texting, Madi reading, me staring into uncertainty.

* * *

I didn't think Mom would be home when I got back from school. But the dentist's office where she works the front desk on Mondays closed up early. There's a blizzard coming.

So there she is when I get to our unit on the second floor. She's taking pictures of everything broken around the apartment. She wants to send them to our landlord all in one go. Not that it's worth it. He never fixes anything, even though he lives right downstairs. We're supposed to feel lucky to live here. Grateful to even be in this town.

I'm not feeling it. Our old rental was cramped, sure. But the landlord there wasn't useless. When the washer broke last year, our current landlord was no help. We had to pay the repair guy ourselves, even though it's not our property. And that's not the end of the problems with the apartment. The back burner on the stove hasn't worked in years. The bathroom ceiling has this nasty mold. The shower's water pressure is so low that it's barely a trickle. That problem needs a video to show.

I wait for Mom to finish filming. There's one bathroom in the unit, and I need some privacy. But it can wait.

Watching the showerhead sputter and give up, I think: *What if I'm pregnant?*

Mom was sixteen when she was pregnant with me. At first, her parents wanted her to give me up for adoption. She said no. So they rushed to sign the papers so she could marry Dad. Almost pushed her down the aisle. You wouldn't think that would be legal in the twenty-first century. But they figured that was best. Best for their respectable, churchgoing lives.

Mom's divorced now. She doesn't talk to her parents. It's just the two of us, mostly, and the late child support checks. Dad's got a new wife and a new kid. He never calls. I'm all Mom's got. Me and too many bills and the rent on this lousy apartment.

Moving to this small town, hours away from our old home in Milwaukee, was supposed to be our big break. New county, new life. Mom said *less crime, better neighborhood*. I wasn't sold. I liked our old neighborhood. I didn't think *suburban* meant *better*. But she talked about the high school. More clubs, more AP courses, smaller class sizes. I was going into ninth grade.

And I understood. This was for me. I was going to go to college, like she never got to. Because she had me. But I was going to be worth it.

This is where I am instead. Hoping Mom doesn't question me taking my backpack into the bathroom when she leaves. Sometimes I do that if I bought pads. There's no reason for her to wonder.

It's going to be negative. It's fine.

I spread the instructions out. They crinkle on the floor. The print is tiny. The directions are simple.

I've never done this. Never knew how it worked, except from jokes. It's like a Covid test, but it's not your snot you're testing. One line for negative, two for positive. You don't have to wait fifteen minutes either. The instructions say three.

I start the test. My chest tightens up when I can't find my phone. How will I know if it's been three minutes? The directions say don't wait too long.

My phone is in the wrong pocket of my backpack. *Phew.* Timer set. I watch it count down to the truth. I'm either pregnant, or I'm not. The test is just confirming what's already happened.

Like when we logged in to find out our SAT scores. Madi and Jasleen clutching each other's hands. Danny grinding his teeth. Me way calmer than I thought I'd be.

Whatever score I was getting, I already got.

* * *

The timer hits zero. I look down at the stick again. I've been careful not to peek.

Two lines. They hit like a physical blow.

I hear myself scream.

Someone knocks on the door. Mom. Of course it's Mom. "Ashley, are you okay? Ashley?"

I think about hiding it. No point. I won't be able to hide it forever.

I am eighteen, a senior in high school, an adult. I feel like a five-year-old who's made a mess she can't clean up.

I twist open the lock. Before I can say anything, Mom takes in the spread-out leaflet on the floor. The stick I'm still clutching in my hand.

Something passes across her face before she can hide it. A look of bone-deep weariness. Disappointment.

After all her efforts, I still didn't escape.

CHAPTER 2

"Well." Mom gulps her feelings down. I see the effort. What it takes not to say, *How could you?* "We can go to Illinois to get this taken care of."

Everything's too fast. No time to think. No space to breathe. Tiny bathroom. Walls of cracked off-white tile closing in. Mom blocking the doorway.

I need to get out.

I barrel toward the door. Mom jumps to one side like a car's speeding toward her. Reaches out a hand to me. I slip through her fingers. But there's nowhere to go. I can't run from my own body.

So I stop. I turn. Mom's swallowing back tears. Barely keeping it together.

"Ashley. I'm not going to tell you what to do. I will never do to you what my mother did to me. Okay? I want you to have options."

Her awkward arms rise for a hug but stop halfway. I can hear her stifled breaths as she holds back from breaking. I can't deal with it. Her feelings. Her memories. The way the second line on that test haunts her.

The past is too close. The past that led to me.

In just three minutes, "probably nothing" became "something." Something too big and real to handle.

"I don't want to rush you," Mom says. "It's just easier, the earlier you decide. Later is harder."

I know. I get it.

When the Supreme Court ruling happened in June this year, Jasleen was furious about it. *Dobbs*. Then the abortion ban in our state. A law brought back from 1849. She kept yelling the year in disbelief. Madi said, "I never knew you could have a zombie law. A law that's undead." Despite her sense of humor, Madi was just as upset. The next time I was at her house, a protest sign was leaning against her bookshelf. *Bans Off Our Bodies.*

I thought a lot about my mom then. How she'd had no choice. Not really. Even when it was legal. I thought about girls like her. Girls whose parents controlled their bodies and their futures.

I didn't think about me.

Then came July, and the sweetness of summer romance. I was a camp counselor at the rec center. Danny Morales served ice cream around the corner, near my bus stop. One day, Lakes of Cream had free samples. I came in for a cold spoonful of blue moon ice cream. I came out feeling warm and shivery at once. Danny asked me out a week later.

And now it's December. A real Wisconsin winter. Frost on the ground. Wet. Cold.

"I need to go for a walk. I can't think like this."

"It's going to snow tonight," Mom says.

"I'll wear boots."

She looks at me, worried. "Don't disappear on me."

As if I'd just walk into a blizzard and keep going. And they'd find me in the morning, icicle stiff. For a second, though, that feels like a relief. If I were dead, I wouldn't have to deal with this.

Come on, Ashley, get real. That's not a solution.

"I'll take my phone," I say. "I'll be back in half an hour."

Mom is careful not to get in my space. Unusually careful. She doesn't hover while I pull on my boots and winter coat. I adjust my gloves. I can't find the fleece headband for my ears. Looking will take too long. So on goes the ugly hat with the earflaps. I hate it. Yellow and orange stripes, with a stupid pompom on top. Makes me look like a kid.

Mr. Harrison, the landlord, is coming in the front of the building as I leave. We almost collide, and he shakes his head.

"Sorry," I call back as he disappears into his ground-floor unit.

I lock the front door behind me because Mr. Harrison gets mad if we forget. Then I rush outside like the cold air means freedom.

We live on the edge of town. Lots of trees here. Maples with bare branches. Big white oaks with dead brown leaves clinging on. A gust of wind rips some off.

The storm is coming.

I don't know what to do. Mom's waiting for me to make up my mind. But it's all so new and big.

Not big, I think. *Tiny. It only just started growing.*

How can something so small loom so large like this?

I stop at the corner and turn around. Halfway back home, I turn again. When I pace at home, Mom jokes, "Don't wear a hole in the carpet." I feel as trapped out here as inside. Just more alone. All that open space, and nowhere to go. What I'm running from is inside me.

I pull out my phone. Right glove off so I can open Snapchat. The cold makes me clumsy. The text I send Madi is full of typos. I don't know when she'll see it. The app doesn't tell you if your friends are online.

I don't want to text Jasleen though. Not after what happened at lunch. She would hate having to hide this from Danny. She's known him since kindergarten. She'd want me to tell him. Right away. And I can't.

Madi won't push me. She knows what it's like to keep a secret. I've done the same for her. We got each other through the pandemic. Her texts and Zoom calls kept me sane. She told me she was bi before she came out to her family. When she was out of school for weeks getting treatment for anxiety and self-harm, I lied to the whole class for her. We look out for each other.

Madelyn is typing. I wait. The fingers of my right hand get red from the wind. Then the phone starts ringing. She's calling me instead.

"Oh my god, Ash, are you okay?" Before I can answer: "Sorry, that's a stupid question. Do you, like, need me to come over? Are you alone right now? When does your mom get home?"

"She was there. She got off work early. She knows."

"Okay, um. Yeah."

"Yeah," I say, and we're both quiet.

"You can come over here if you need to, you know," Madi offers.

She keeps forgetting I don't have my own car. I can't just take Mom's without asking. And the bus doesn't go where Madi lives. It's a new development. Everyone there has a two-car garage. No one rents.

"Can you pick me up?"

"I'll be there in ten."

I text Mom where I'll be. The wind picks up, but I don't go back inside. I just stand next to the wall of the building. The first flakes are coming down. Not enough to make driving scary. It's just a ten-minute ride.

Ten minutes away and a different world.

CHAPTER 3

When I was a kid, I saw *The Firebird*. Not live onstage. They were playing a recording of it at the library one summer. I wanted to be the ballerina with the scarlet headdress. I waved my arms just like her, almost knocking a book display over. I tried going on the tips of my toes in my sneakers. The librarian said I'd hurt myself. Said I needed proper classes. She told my mom about the Milwaukee Ballet School & Academy.

Like we could ever afford *those* fees. When fall came, Mom found me a dance class in the Before and After public school program. I had to do something till she came home from work, after all. I learned to dance, even if it wasn't ballet like I wanted. I'd never be the Firebird, spinning in her red tutu. But that was fine. You can't have everything in life.

Madi did seven years of ballet. Then she stopped

because of how her teacher pressured the girls not to gain weight. It was messing with her head. And I get it. Telling thirteen-year-olds that? Not cool.

It's just . . . I never even got to start. I was out before lesson one.

I try hard not to be jealous of Madi for being rich. She never rubs it in. But when her car pulls up, newer than any my mom's ever owned . . .

Well. The first thing I think is that if Madi got knocked up, she wouldn't have to think about her parents' bank account. About how much going to Illinois will set us back. About how much more it would cost to have the baby.

For all the talk of choice, I don't know if I have one. My mom would never decide this for me. No matter how disappointed she is. She wouldn't make me do what she thinks is right, the way her parents did. They acted like she'd go to hell if she didn't do what they said. That's why she hasn't talked to them in years.

But she doesn't have to say anything like that to me. There just isn't enough money, and I know it.

Madi gets out of the car and pulls me into a bear hug. For a moment, I don't think about money. I let myself drift. She opens the side door, and I get in. The windshield wipers lull me into a daze. Snowflakes hit the glass, melt, get brushed away. Madi focuses on the road. I watch the snow fall.

When we get out, I realize I don't have my stuff. No pj's or toothbrush. No clean clothes. I hope tomorrow's a virtual learning day. The thing we have now instead of snow days.

Madi makes up some excuse for her parents. *We have a project due tomorrow. We're going to work on it in my room.* I nod along on autopilot. *Hi, Mr. Wendt. Hi, Mrs. Wendt.* It's nice not to have to think right now. Someone else will take care of things.

Madi leads me upstairs and into her room. Books are everywhere. When we started hanging out freshman year, she had every single Cassandra Clare book. Now her tastes are broader. She lets me borrow anything I want.

I check out the books on her desk. Like I'm browsing at a library. Hardcovers, recent, the front flaps marking her place. *She Who Became the Sun. Poster Girl.*

I don't know what that one's about, but I think of the posters in the nurse's office. Smiling couples who use protection, and it works. They stare out from the pictures: thoughtful, confident, safe. The opposite of me.

I am not a poster girl for anything. More like a warning ad for what not to do. Every step that got me here seemed fine at the time. And now here I am. Pregnant by a guy I dumped and haven't talked to since.

"Do you want to talk about it?" Madi's voice cuts through.

I used to ask her that, when her mental health was at its worst. Now she's the one talking carefully to me. Not wanting to push. Wondering how bad it is.

I hate this so much.

"Does anyone else know?" she goes on. "Besides your mom, I mean. I don't want to accidentally—"

"Don't tell Jasleen."

Madi nods, understanding what I didn't say. That Danny doesn't know yet.

"I just found out. I'm not ready." I don't know why I keep talking. Like I have to justify myself. But then it starts pouring out of me. All the stuff I couldn't say to my mom, I can say to my best friend. She won't judge me. And I need to tell someone how scared I am. How overwhelmed. "I don't know what to say. I don't want to be stuck with him. What if he's like my dad? I can't handle that. I can't handle this! How is this real? I already applied to college. This can't be happening. It can't. I was going to have a life!"

Madi grabs my arm. "Ashley, your life isn't over! You'll get through this."

I don't want fake comfort. I pull away too fast, knocking the pile of books to the floor. "You don't get it! None of this is okay! I'm going to end up just like my mom."

I'm gasping. This isn't supposed to be happening. Any of it.

"You're not your mom, and Danny isn't your dad."

"Stop telling me it's going to be fine! It's not. It's a mess now! My whole life!" I can't breathe. I try to focus. *Breathe in. Breathe out.* Like I would tell Madi if she had a panic attack.

It doesn't help. The more I try to breathe, the less air I get.

Now I see fear in Madi's face too. She's also freaked out. I sit down on the bed, dizzy. I think I'm going to faint.

"Are you okay? Oh my god. Breathe."

I try to say, "I can't." It doesn't sound like anything.

Madi runs out of the room. I hear something rattling in the bathroom. I don't know what she's looking for. Being alone is worse. I can't get enough air. It feels like forever.

The door bursts open. Madi has a glass of water. And something else she presses into my hand.

"Take this. It helps if you're panicking."

I don't look at the pill. I swallow it and the whole glass of water.

Whatever it was, it can't have kicked in yet. But I already feel a little better. Maybe drinking something helped. I sit there and wait, quiet. Madi watches me. She's trying to project a sense of calm, but I can sense she's worried.

Eventually, I get calmer too. Then I get sleepier. I curl up like a kid taking a nap.

CHAPTER 4

Mom is shaking me awake. Too much bright light. Mouth all gross. Maybe I ate some bad leftovers? I feel so groggy. How is it time for school already? When did I go to sleep?

"Ashley? I'm so sorry. Please wake up. Please."

That's Madi's voice. It all comes back. I'm not at home. I'm pregnant, and my life is over.

The thought doesn't freak me out. I feel weirdly chill.

At least in my mind. My body—it's like the time I had two beers fast. And on an empty stomach. I woke up with the worst headache.

It was August 2021, and all of us were sick of the pandemic. Finally double vaxxed. In-person school was opening again. We'd been cooped up since spring of freshman year. That summer, we went wild.

A little too wild. A ton of people caught Covid that night. I thought I had too, and warned everyone I might be sick. Nope, it was a hangover. I was so embarrassed. The lightweight jokes got old fast. I haven't gotten drunk again since.

"Madi?" I croak. Open my eyes, close them. Adjust to the light. Open them again.

"Oh, thank god!" Madi looks awful. I can tell she didn't get any sleep. I know what her face looks like when she's splashed it with water to hide the streaks from tears. "I wasn't supposed to give that to you. I'm sorry. You were so upset, and I just . . . didn't think."

"It's okay," I say. I'm not sure what she gave me. I took something last night, right? Maybe I shouldn't have. But it's hard to be upset about anything. I'm so relaxed. I stretch, stand up slowly, and head to the bathroom. Wash my face. Put toothpaste on my finger. I forgot my toothbrush. My stomach's not great, but whatever. At least I'm not throwing up.

Madi's still all tense when I get back. She's changed her clothes, but she's even more of a mess than me.

"Were you up all night?" I ask.

"I was looking it up online. The Xanax. My psych said it's illegal to share, but . . . I didn't think one pill was so bad? And then I remembered you were . . . remembered what you told me. And like, all the rules are different. If you're pregnant."

Something cuts through the fog of calm.

"What do you mean? Can it hurt the . . . ?"

Why do I care? Wouldn't it be a good thing if I miscarried now? Just a heavy period a few weeks late. A lucky chance. No decisions to make. No future to worry over.

Except that's not how I feel.

Madi takes a deep breath. "It's Category D. Like, they can still give it to you when you're pregnant. But it's risky. They'd rather use something else if they can."

I don't know what that category means. But I do know "a doctor can give it to you if you need it" is different from what just happened. I feel like an idiot.

"You didn't even tell me what it was." I didn't ask either. But come on. *Xanax?* Everyone knows that's heavy stuff. Last year, one girl got busted for selling hers online. I don't know why she would. If you have enough money to see a psych and get meds, you probably don't need extra cash.

That girl got probation. Less than a Black kid back in Milwaukee would get. I live in this super white suburb now, but I still know that.

"I'm sorry. I thought it would help."

"I'm not mad," I say. But I realize I am. Mad at both of us. At Madi, for being so stupid. This isn't like underage drinking. She gave me her pill when I was freaking out and not thinking. *Illegally.* And now she tells me it's bad for the . . . baby? . . . fetus? . . . pregnancy? I don't want to think about how I feel about what's inside me. Or why I'm so upset. I just wish she'd never looked the medicine up. It's not just sleeping in my clothes that makes me feel gross now. Dirty.

I can't blame it all on her. She was worried about me. She gave me the same thing she'd take if she had a panic attack. And I just went along with it.

That's my whole problem, isn't it?

When Danny suggested we have sex the first time, I

drifted along. Let him take the lead. He bought condoms, so I didn't think about getting my own birth control. Now look where I am.

When Madi gave me her Xanax, it looked like a solution. I didn't ask any questions. I just swallowed it down. Even yesterday, when Jasleen didn't understand how hard it was for me to see Danny at our lunch table, I didn't say anything.

And now I'm probably going to have an abortion. There's no point worrying if I took a drug I shouldn't have. What difference does it make? Pretty soon, I won't be pregnant anymore. I know what my mom wants, and I don't know what I want. So I guess I'll do what she wants.

But I should have a better reason than that. I should have a better reason for a lot of the things I do.

CHAPTER 5

The snow didn't stick, so school's still on. Madi and I don't talk in the car. I'm still yawning and fuzzy when we get to school. I'm not usually this tired in the morning.

Señora Díaz notices I don't turn in my homework.

AP Spanish is my best class. I might be in "dumb math," as the AP Calculus crowd calls it, but I'm good at languages. After the Borges presentation I did, Sofia Ical asked me what country my family was from. She didn't believe I learned Spanish in school. And Danny went, "Nah, she doesn't speak it at home. She just studies that hard!"

That was back when we were together.

Now I make something up so Señora Díaz won't bother me. My backpack is still at home. The short story questions I was supposed to answer are in there, blank. I don't even have the textbook with me.

"I know you turned in your college application ahead

of the deadline, Ashley. But the AP exam isn't till May. Stay on top of things. No senioritis in this class."

Let her think it's senioritis. I don't want her to know the truth. She wrote my rec letter for the University of Wisconsin. I paid the extra fee to apply to the flagship Madison campus too. They have so many different language classes. Señora Díaz helped me out when I stumbled over the first-gen question. My mom's parents went to college. My parents didn't. Because they had me.

The teacher moves on, swooping in on anyone with their phones still out. Danny, as usual. Probably on Discord again. That's another thing that annoyed me when we were dating. He was always on his phone, or his souped-up computer. Talking to people I didn't know and he'd never seen. Obsessing over *Elden Ring*. That was his main social life. Sure, he had friends at school too. But he mainly talked to them about gaming.

Me? The pandemic hit halfway through freshman year. Just when I'd finally gotten to know a few people in this town. I hated being cooped up at home alone. Mom still had to work, and she needed the car. I got way too familiar with the walls of our house and the sidewalks nearby. As soon as I could start seeing people in real life again, I did.

It was different for Danny. He didn't spend lockdown alone. He had the twins climbing up the walls. His little brother and sister—they're in fourth grade now. Meanwhile, his gamer friends were all ages and didn't constantly need something. They became his lifeline. And he always put them first. *Including* ahead of me, until I got sick of it.

No way is Danny Morales ready to be a dad. He could be a fun older brother. A cool uncle. But being a parent isn't a game. My dad wasn't ready for the reality of it. He'd thought he was. But when things got tough, he was around less and less. Until he wasn't around at all.

* * *

Jasleen and I are in the same math class. Last-period Precalculus on slow mode. She always jokes about how she's proof not all Indians are good at math.

She can tell something's wrong. It's pretty obvious. My

clothes look slept in. I tried to fix my hair in the bathroom, but it's still messy. Not to mention I don't have my textbook. Jasleen can't ask me what happened because the teacher keeps droning on. Freezing rain hammers on the window outside.

I do the math. Not the one being taught. The one that matters. Even if I got a full ride, how could I go to college with a baby? Who would look after it? What am I supposed to do, go straight from the hospital to freshman orientation?

If I go through with it, the baby will be born in August. I picture it, wrapped in a blanket. With a wrinkled old-man face, like all babies have when they're born. Wrinkles that smooth out to baby fat.

I shouldn't even be thinking about this. I'm not ready to have a kid. Last night proved it. What kind of mother would I be? I'm not even mature enough to take care of myself. My mother works herself to the bone to make rent so I can go to this school. It's not just that I'm afraid of letting her down. Throwing her hard work away.

It's that I don't think I can live her life.

I can have kids later. When I'm a grown-up on more than just paper.

It's just . . . if I don't want to have the baby, why am I trying so hard to convince myself I can't have it?

*　*　*

Jasleen catches my arm as soon as the bell rings.

"Look, I'm sorry about yesterday. Are you going to be at practice tonight? We should talk."

Talk is the last thing I want to do. If I don't, though, she'll think I'm holding a grudge.

"I don't think the Y's going to be open," I stall. "Have you seen the weather?" The storm that didn't come yesterday is definitely on for today.

"Oh, yeah. Duh. I guess dance class is off for sure." She still looks uneasy. Like she wants to ask me what's going on.

I tell her a half truth.

"I had a bad fight with my mom. That's why I'm in a mood." Okay, it's mostly a lie. But close enough.

Jasleen gives me a hug. I'm stiff at first, then I relax. It's way too early for her to feel a bump.

I wish I could tell her the truth. She knows a lot about this stuff. In May, she was telling me about Texas and their six-week ban. She said six weeks pregnant is really four weeks after you have sex. The first two weeks are from your last period.

I didn't know that. There's a lot of stuff I don't know. Mom says the longer you wait, the more the abortion costs. I know at some point it's too late.

I should start looking things up. This isn't a school project I can put off till the night before. I can't afford to drift right now.

CHAPTER 6

At home, I shut myself in my room and pull out my Chromebook. I start searching the internet and taking notes. It feels like I'm doing a research project. Like the one I did for AP Spanish. Except I'm not looking up facts about a dead genius Argentinian writer. I'm looking up facts about my own body.

Let's see . . . it's normal for the breasts to feel sore around week six. I thought my bra just didn't fit right. Also, it's actually week seven now. You count by the week that's beginning. Not the one that just ended.

Week seven is also when morning sickness might start. It's usually worst in week nine.

The little growing thing is called an embryo right now. In week eight, it will become a fetus. It's only the size of a large bean at that point. But it will graduate to that next stage. Like the pre-K kids "graduating" to kindergarten.

They didn't do that when I was going into kindergarten. It makes me laugh.

"You've got a long way to go, little bean," I say out loud. Then I feel weird about talking to it.

Most miscarriages happen before week twelve. Because of that, a lot of women hide their pregnancy in the first few months. Even if they got pregnant on purpose.

So I can't start thinking of it as a cute little bean. Even if I keep it, I might lose it.

I close that tab and look up Illinois. I click on a couple of pages I think are abortion clinics. But they turn out to be crisis pregnancy centers wanting to talk me out of it. Eventually, I find a couple of real clinics near Wisconsin.

Mom knocks on the door.

"Come in." Mom is always careful about my privacy. She never just barges in. I wonder if she wishes she'd given me less space now. Seeing what I did with it.

But she let me go to Madi's yesterday. She trusts me to always come back home. So I don't flip the laptop shut like I sometimes do. I try to trust her back.

Mom sees what I'm looking at. The open tabs of clinic pages.

"Do you want me to help you make an appointment?"

I shake my head. I'm not ready to commit. I don't know what I'm waiting for. What will make me be ready. "I've got time, right? As long as it's still legal."

Mom sighs. She looks at me like my Precalculus teacher did last month. When it was clear I'd missed what a tangent was and faked my way through two weeks before asking.

"After ten weeks, they can't give you pills. The procedure gets more complicated and expensive the further along you are. With so many people coming from out of state due to the bans, they might not have an appointment if you wait. At least not in a reasonable time."

Right. She told me it would cost more if I waited. It was almost the first thing she said when she found out.

I try to look up the next appointment at one clinic. The website doesn't list available dates and times. I guess they have to be careful. They don't want someone coming in to shoot the doctor.

I would have to send them a request to see when appointments are. That feels too much like a decision. I am not ready yet.

I look up from the keyboard and see my mother's tired face.

My mom loves me. She always puts me first. And she would not have chosen to give birth to me if her voice had been the one that counted.

She has never said it. Never would, not in a million years. But the way she's fighting to save me from her own life makes it clear. I know she wonders who she could have been, if not for me.

She loves me. I'm also something that was done to her. Not something she chose.

It's a strange thing to feel. To know she wants to do better by me than her parents ever did by her. To see how hard she's trying, through her own trauma. She's making sure I have the facts, but she's not forcing me.

I'm thankful for her.

I really am.

So I don't ask her if she wanted me, then. It would be cruel. And I already know the answer.

But I need her to give me space. Just knowing how she feels is its own pressure.

"I need more time to think, Mom. I get that you want to help me, but I have to think it through myself."

Mom looks like she wants to say something. But whatever it is, she holds back.

* * *

The next day, we're snowed in together. The storm came after all. I log on to virtual school. Mom shovels a path around her car. She doesn't ask me to help. I don't offer. I'm not sure if I'm allowed to or not. If it might hurt the little bean. Like when I tried growing a lima bean in a bag in fourth grade. The rest of the class did it. Mine never sprouted.

CHAPTER 7

I'm the only customer at Lakes of Cream after school on Friday. After the blizzard last week, not many people want ice cream. And most of those who do want it are getting burgers and frozen custard at Culver's.

Most of the workers are packing up orders for restaurants. Someone's getting a ton of the blue moon flavor. It used to be my favorite. I'm not sure I like it anymore.

The guy minding the cash register is on his phone.

"Hey, how're you doing?" I say. No answer. He looks at me like I'm ruining his break. Rude. "Is Danny Morales here?"

"No."

The counter guy goes back to ignoring me. My courage slips away.

I could just message Danny. He would like that better.

He always preferred talking online. It gave him more time to think through his response, he said.

When we had the big breakup fight, I saw what he meant. He lashed out hard when he felt cornered. There was no edit button in person.

Okay, maybe this was a dumb idea. Madi said it was better to get it over with. That honesty pays off. But what does she know? I know Danny's going to react badly if I spring it on him like this.

Right. Time to go. I skipped dance practice to be here. What a waste.

"Thanks," I say to the counter guy, even though he didn't do anything. I turn and leave, brushing against the plastic sign with the shop's cheesy logo. A tiny lake made of ice cream, with a motorboat zooming by. The wake behind it is patterned like a waffle cone.

That always bugged me. The lake in this town is a no-motor lake. The art shows a boat you would never see here.

It's easier to think about that than anything important. I feel tired all the time now.

I sit on the bench outside the shop. I'm trying to figure out when the next bus comes. Then a family passes behind me to go inside. I look up out of reflex and see Danny holding the door open for the twins. Elena has pigtails, and Jake's curly hair is getting long. They are begging for chocolate ice cream—no, mint chocolate chip—no, a banana split with chocolate sauce.

"We're just here to pick up my paperwork," Danny explains. "If you're good, you can have an ice cream sandwich when we get home. But not if you whine, okay?"

Jake stops demanding ice cream and walks into the shop. Elena is less impressed with Danny's promise.

"Let's go home now! I don't care about your stupid paperwork," she says. Full-on nine-year-old bratty.

Danny shakes his head, looks up, and spots me. He freezes. We're stuck, each pinned by the other's gaze. Held together when neither of us wants to be.

I'm going to tell him. I'm right about to. But little Elena runs back to the sidewalk while her brother is distracted. Danny turns away to catch her. He grabs her arm as she reaches the curb. She was steps away from the busy intersection.

"Do *not* scare me like that, Elena. The cars here are out of control!"

"I wasn't going to run into the street," she lies.

"Really?" Danny clearly doesn't believe her, but he's more relaxed now that she's stopped trying to run away. He keeps a hold on her wrist though.

"I would have looked both ways first."

It's the silliest thing I've heard in a while, and I laugh out loud. I wonder what it's like to have younger brothers and sisters. To watch a baby become a toddler. A toddler become a kid.

Danny herds Elena back to the shop. As he passes by my bench, he sees I'm still watching.

"What are you staring at? You're the one who broke up with me," he says bitterly.

I try to get out what I need to say. But it's swallowed up by fear. After his harsh words, I've lost my nerve. And now I look desperate and weird, showing up at his work like this. I say nothing.

Jake opens the door of the ice cream shop. "Where is everybody? Elena? Danny?"

"Come on," Danny tells Elena, and they go inside with Jake. The door clangs shut behind them. A cold sound on a cold day.

I should be upset. After we broke up, I cried for days. He was the first person I dated. I don't count Hunter in middle school. He and I ate lunch together for a few days and "broke up" after two weeks. Danny was something different. Something real.

And now it's over, broken beyond repair. The shy warm feelings are gone. I don't even want to try getting back together. I know one thing for sure from my parents' story. Being pregnant doesn't suddenly make marrying your high school crush a good idea.

But watching him with his brother and sister, I can see he's not my dad. I'd forgotten this in the time since we broke up. How careful he is with them. How loving. He could be a good father. I think that if he knew, he'd want to.

Then it flashes in front of me again. The scorn and hurt on his face. The judgment in his voice. The stinging words.

It's so cold out. I walk to the bus stop, wishing I had my own car. I can feel the wind through my gloves.

I should have used the bathroom before I left school. My uterus is pressing on something. The ride home feels way longer than it is.

With my body changing already, how long can I keep this a secret?

CHAPTER 8

I toss and turn that night. Pick up my phone. Put it back. Put on my slippers to leave my room. Stop in the doorway. Go back to bed. Fail to fall asleep.

At some point, I pass out.

On Saturday, I wake up calm. Knowing.

It's early in the morning, and Mom is sleeping in. She doesn't usually get a full weekend. Her job at the dentist's office isn't full time, so she picks up remote call center hours too. She's got a shift today, but it starts at eleven. At least she doesn't have to drive anywhere.

I'll tell her after her shift.

I am going to have the baby. I am going to prove them all wrong. Everyone who thinks I can't do this. Myself too. For this little bean, I can be a good mother.

It's scary to think about. Me as a mom. Me as an adult.

It's like I'm standing on the edge of the lake at the

beginning of summer, when it's still cold. About to take the plunge. Except after this jump, there's no climbing back out. A kid is forever.

I still feel like a kid. I've let my own mother shield me as much as she can. She's kept us afloat so long that I forgot how one mistake is the difference between getting by and being desperate. It's been a long time since we were desperate. But I remember. During the divorce. I was just old enough to notice. Way too young to help. We weren't struggling then. We were drowning. We spent a month in a homeless shelter.

Me having a kid is exactly the kind of thing that could push us back.

But the divorce gave Mom her freedom. Some things are worth it. And this is one of them. I can't explain why. I just know. If I don't have this kid, I will always, always wonder. I'll have that question at the back of my mind: *Did I give up on my baby because I didn't think I had what it took? Because I didn't believe in myself?*

A fierce confidence fills me. I can have this baby.

I will. I'm going to be the best parent I can be. I won't be perfect. But I've known my whole life that perfect doesn't happen. I'll be what my kid needs. What matters more than impossible perfection. I'll be *there*.

* * *

The high of having decided lasts half an hour. I know what I want to do. I feel my choice as a calm, still place at the heart of me. But I get nervous passing my mom's bedroom door. She's catching up on sleep while she can. I'll tell her later. I will.

I press on my belly to calm myself. There's no bump anyone else can see yet. But I can feel a little swelling, a little firmness. By graduation, everyone will know. I'll be walking across the stage seven months pregnant. The girl parents warn about. The bad example. The one you don't want your college-bound daughter hanging out with.

So what. *So what?* I'll show them. I'll show everyone.

But I need to tell someone to make it real.

* * *

I wait till Mom is working with her door closed to log on

to the video call. I use my headphones and keep my voice down, the way I always do so I don't disturb Mom during her shift.

Except this time, I'm also trying to keep her from hearing. She doesn't spy, but you can't help noticing a loud conversation in the next room.

I'm the only one on Zoom. Then Jasleen pops up. Madi texts that she'll be there in ten. So it's me sitting awkwardly with Jasleen, who doesn't know. Whom I didn't tell I was pregnant in the first place. Who's noticed me skipping dance practice and acting weird.

Maybe it's a good thing Madi's late.

I plunge into the uneasy silence. "You probably know I've been . . . keeping something secret."

Jasleen nods. She's not muted, but she might as well be. No sound at all.

"You can't tell Danny. I need to tell him on my own time."

Another nod. Her forehead creases, puzzled.

That edge of the lake feeling again. *Jump, jump, jump!* You can't stand on the shore forever.

"I'm pregnant. And I'm going to have the baby."

Jasleen can't hide her shock. She didn't expect that to be my secret. I'm going to have to keep doing this. Telling Danny will be worse.

But right now, I don't feel afraid. For the first time since the condom broke, I feel like I'm in control. Powerful. A firebird spreading wings of flame.

Madi logs on, and we all spin a story. Of who this kid will be. Of everything I'll do for them. Jasleen thinks of practical things. Hospitals, insurance, doctors. Madi promises to read to the baby as soon as they're old enough to understand anything. To teach them colors and shapes out of books.

"What will you name it?" Jasleen asks.

"I haven't figured that out," I say. "I call them Little Bean right now. I don't even know if I should be thinking about boy or girl names. The doctors didn't do the test yet."

Madi points out, "Kids don't always keep the names you give them. Or stay the gender you thought they were."

I see how true that is in my own life. I'm not trans, but I want to change the name I was given as a baby. I hate using my last name. Muller, for my dad. Someday, I'll change it to Hoffman, for my mom. I don't want to give my kid the name Muller. I hope Little Bean won't feel the same way someday about Morales. I hope they'll feel good about who their parents are.

"I wonder who our parents thought we were going to be," Jasleen says. "It's not just names or gender. You can't predict *anything* about a kid's future. Their life won't go according to your plans."

Madi snorts. Her parents' expectations weigh on her. Not just to succeed. They want her to be someone she's not. Less anxious, less queer, less nerdy, less weird.

"I think that's cool, actually. You give a kid a start, and then they do their own thing. It's kind of like magic. You can be scared of what you can't control," I say. "Or you can love them as their own person."

My mom's parents wanted to control her. I want Little Bean to have the freedom to be whoever they become.

* * *

After the free Zoom cuts off at forty minutes, I have hours left to wait. I'm all keyed up when Mom's shift ends, tense and brave at once. When she comes down to the kitchen to heat up leftovers for dinner, I've already popped them into the microwave. As if that would make a difference. But she smiles when she sees the table already set, the pot of mashed potatoes steaming on the stove. Even though they came out of an instant packet. At least making them was distracting.

"Mom," I say, before I can lose my nerve. "I made up my mind. I'm not going to get an abortion. I want to have this baby."

Her smile gets tighter but doesn't disappear. She holds her face together carefully. She must remember the day of the pregnancy test. One look from her sent me running out of the house. Needing space, air, someone to talk to who wasn't her.

"I was thinking that might be what you chose. Ashley, I'll be here for you no matter what. And your baby. It's going to be hard, but we can do it." She looks not quite at me. At a place over my shoulder. I recognize that look. She's staring down the whole world for me.

CHAPTER 9

Before I know what's happening, we're hugging. We're a small family. We have to stick together. We only have each other.

Then Mom starts giving me directions.

"You need to take prenatal vitamins. The ones with folic acid. And there are forms, for our health care."

Neither of her two jobs has insurance, so we're on a state plan: BadgerCare Plus. Or rather, I'm on it, because I'm still in school. Mom tries not to need health care.

She shows me our account online. How to report if someone on the plan becomes pregnant. "You can fill it out yourself. You're going to have a lot of forms to fill out. It's a good time to start taking that responsibility."

I have been a grown-up, technically anyway, since September. Back then, I had no secrets. I had a boyfriend

I was crazy about, and a plan to get into the state flagship for college. Everything that's happened since then . . .

Yeah. It's not reassuring.

And looking at the online form isn't either. We're supposed to report changes within ten days of when they happen. For a second, I worry there'll be trouble because I waited. Not that I knew I had to do this!

Then I realize that ten days after getting pregnant, the test might not even work yet. And I laugh. I'm not going to let some stupid form scare me.

But as I fill it out, I get queasy. Acid jumps into my throat. Madi says this is how panic feels to her. I can't be panicking. The form is easier than I thought. No worse than a standardized test form. I follow the instructions. I fill out my data. Then Mom signs off, since the account is in her name.

And up come the instant mashed potatoes. I run for the toilet but end up barfing on the bathroom tiles. I'm *not* anxious. The morning sickness has just started. At night.

Mom calls from outside the door, asking if I'm okay, if I need help.

I feel horrible, and my hair is gross and sticky. But I've made my decision. This is what I chose. I wash my face, get some wipes from under the sink, and clean up.

* * *

The first step is the hardest. The next is easier, and the next. A week and a half later, I go to my first appointment. I was lucky to get an appointment before doctors start going away for the winter holidays. All I know about my doctor is that she takes BadgerCare and she's near a bus stop. That means I can get to her office on days Mom drives to work at the dentist.

At the time of my first scan, Mom's working the call center job instead. So I get the car. I drive extra carefully.

Dr. Erickson is middle-aged and judgy. Her eyebrows go up when she sees how young I am. She checks that my vitamins have folic acid. Then she frowns at how late I started them. They're supposed to be started three months *before* getting pregnant, to lower the chance of scary birth defects.

"Well," I point out, "I wasn't exactly planning to get pregnant."

I hoped a joke might break the tension, but nope. Not even the ghost of a smile on her face. Maybe now she thinks I think birth defects are funny. It's a relief to get to the ultrasound room, with the young, friendly tech. Never mind that I have no clue how an ultrasound works. At least the tech looks at me without that judgmental frown.

She talks me through each step, explaining how the scan will show us what's inside my uterus. Inside me. I almost don't mind the weird "wand" she has to stick between my legs. It only hurts a little. And it's less scary with someone explaining.

"Twenty-two millimeters long," the tech says. "About nine weeks."

There it is on the screen. Black and white like an old movie. My first look at Little Bean, who is small, but not very much like a lima bean. I can see the head and cord, though the rest of it looks blurry. The head is more of a shape, a suggestion. This funny-looking first glimpse of my baby makes my stomach flip. In a good way, this time. Jumping for joy.

"I'll print it out for you," the tech says after she finishes. She says Little Bean looks "good." I'm not sure what she was checking, but *good* is definitely good. I miss watching it when the screen goes blank, but the tech brings the picture in quickly.

I go away with more printouts. A list of foods to avoid. No queso fresco for me. No sushi. Not like I'm dining out on seafood at the Japanese restaurant, so that one doesn't matter. A warning about petting stray cats or changing cat litter. That's fine, I don't have a cat. We live in a no-pets apartment. The only printouts I really care about are the one with the due date and date of my next appointment, and the ultrasound picture.

As I get out of the car at home, I see the landlord pulling in. We end up coming in the front door at the same time. Mr. Harrison looks down at the papers I'm carrying.

I think about trying to hide them. But he already saw them, probably. And I won't be ashamed of this. I don't move the ultrasound printout from the top of the stack.

"Congratulations!" he says. Which is what you're supposed to say, but of course no one has said that to me. I wonder why he's being so nice. He usually brushes me off quickly. And that's on a good day. "I don't want to presume . . ."

"Yes, it's mine." Maybe I shouldn't be telling Mr. Harrison this. But why else would I be carrying this around? Besides, he'll find out when I start showing.

"That mold your mother sent a video of . . . it's not good for you in this condition. I'll get that repair done soon. I'll let her know when I've set it up."

He smiles and then heads into his apartment. Maybe the thought of a little baby living here makes him want to speed up repairs? If our landlord actually fixes stuff for a change, I'm not complaining.

CHAPTER 10

After the first rush of confidence, it's a struggle to keep up with everything. I have homework, midterms, medical stuff, planning for the future. Jasleen asks if I'm coming back to the YWCA dance group. The coach asked Jasleen if she should take my name off the list. I've missed too many practices to be in the next show.

It hurts to admit I'm not going back. But something has to give. I call the YWCA and tell them I'm dropping out. That saves the spring semester fees that would start in January. Soon money will be tighter than it's been in a while. This is the right choice.

It feels like the end of my childhood though. I tell myself that I'll have other chances to dance. But I know the truth. I won't have time. Little Bean will be sick, or there'll be no one to watch them. It will be all I can do just to keep up with my responsibilities. There won't be room for everything I once wanted.

* * *

When school lets out for winter break, I crash. Midterms are over. Christmas is this Sunday. I have no responsibilities this weekend and nowhere to be.

Madi is in Florida with her family, and Jasleen is visiting her grandparents in India. My mom signed up for a call center shift on Christmas. They pay extra if you work on a holiday. So we move Christmas to Saturday.

We wouldn't have gone to a service either way. After the divorce, Mom left the conservative Lutheran church she grew up in. We only go to churches for weddings and funerals.

But Christmas is still a big deal in our family. We have a mini tree, only a foot tall, but it's real and not plastic. We decorate it with tiny ornaments. They're mostly reused beads from costume jewelry. But we also have a star on top. When I was nine, Mom helped me make it out of glitter glue and cardboard. I imagine showing my child how to do craft projects. Guiding their hand so they don't send glitter glue splattering onto the table.

It's cold outside, and chilly even indoors. Gas prices are up, so the heating is not turned up as high as last winter. Mom suggests watching a movie. I grab my computer and a bunch of blankets. We try watching a free Christmas movie. But it's clear after five minutes that some movies are free for a reason. I show Mom a YouTube recording of *The Nutcracker* instead. Mom claps at the end as if the dancers could hear us.

"That was adorable. What was the ballet you liked when you were little? The one with the bird?" she asks.

"*The Firebird*." I have it bookmarked, so it's easy to find. But I'm a bit shy about sharing it. *The Firebird* is my favorite, the one that got me into dance. Now that I'm not dancing anymore, it's somehow even more personal.

We watch as Prince Ivan chases the Firebird, a creature out of Russian legend. She's played by a dancer all in red, with red feathers in her pinned-up hair. The prince catches her. For a moment, the Firebird is trapped. She trades a single feather for her freedom, promising to help Prince Ivan in a time of need.

After the Firebird disappears, the story shifts. Prince Ivan falls in love with a beautiful princess. But she's under a spell, trapped by the monster Koschei. She and twelve other princesses are held in his castle. Koschei can never die, and he keeps his prisoners in a magical trance.

When Koschei shows up, Prince Ivan uses the feather to call for help. The Firebird arrives in all her glory. She forces Koschei and his servants to dance till they collapse and fall asleep. The Firebird tells Ivan to destroy the secret egg that Koschei hides his soul in. Prince Ivan crushes the egg, and Koschei the Deathless . . . dies. The sun rises, and all of Koschei's servants are freed.

The ballet is all about freedom, really. If Prince Ivan had kept the Firebird caged, instead of letting her go, he wouldn't have been a hero. He would have had no feather to call on for help to defeat Koschei. And so the prince would have ended up just another prisoner.

CHAPTER 11

On January 1, we ring in 2023. I go back to school feeling rested from the break. Ready to take on the new year.

What happens next blindsides me.

Mr. Harrison knocks on our door. When my mom answers, he tells her that we're going to have to move out during repairs. No, he doesn't know when they'll be finished. But the work is starting in two days, so we better make plans.

Mom is baffled. Outraged.

"You can't kick us out with this little notice. Those repairs can be done during the day, when we're out of the house. I've always paid my rent on time and never made any trouble here. Let's work something out."

"Well, you see," says Mr. Harrison, "your daughter shouldn't be exposed to that type of mold when she's pregnant. It's not healthy." He looks over Mom's shoulder at me. I glare back. He tries to sound all friendly. But he's fake to the core. "It would be so awful if anything happened. I could get sued! I can't have that hanging over me."

Mom spins around, looks at me. I know she's wondering how he knows, when I'm not even showing yet.

The landlord continues talking to her back. "I'll get all those other issues fixed too. All those photos you've been bombarding me with. It will take longer, but you wanted them seen to."

And this was the guy congratulating me before. What a piece of work.

Mom gets out of the conversation as quickly as possible and closes the door.

"How does he know?" she yells as soon as he's gone.

"He . . . he saw my ultrasound printout when we were coming in at the same time. After my first appointment." I feel humiliated now, conned. I knew what he was like. And yet I took him at his word. "Can he do this?"

Mom sighs. "I wish you'd told me. Things have been tense with him. After I asked him to do repairs, he said he would raise the rent starting in June. We can't afford it. I tried to talk him down, but he wants us gone. He's trying to make it so hard to stay that we leave early. The mold and you being pregnant are just an excuse. But I wish he hadn't found out."

I'm not sure how I could have stopped it. Turning the printout over? Telling him it was my cousin having a baby? Would that have worked? I didn't know Mr. Harrison was hassling Mom. How could I have known?

"Isn't it discrimination if he evicts us over that? Because I'm pregnant? Isn't that illegal?"

Mom looks at me like I'm the most naïve person on earth.

"Do you have a lawyer you can call? Discrimination happens all the time. The law only helps if you can pay someone to defend your rights for you. Besides, a landlord who wants to force a tenant out can get a lot scarier than this. He's not going to change his mind. We'd better start looking for somewhere else to live. Before he starts thinking about other ways to make us leave."

"It's not fair," I say. I realize I sound like a whiny kid. But this isn't right. There's got to be something we can do.

"When did you start thinking life would be fair? You have to be savvier than this, if you're going to be a mom," she snaps, as if this is my fault. Which it kind of is. My face gets hot, and my eyes sting with tears. Maybe if I'd lied or dodged. Done anything but proudly tell the truth . . .

Mom doesn't notice how upset I am. "I'm going to start making calls to find a new place. We might be couch surfing for a while."

She tries to make it sound like we're not going to be homeless. But I remember that month in the shelter. She thinks I don't because I was only six. We had moved out, and Mom was divorcing my dad. Getting out of a marriage she'd never wanted. We stayed at a friend's house for a bit. But we couldn't stay for long, and Mom couldn't get a rental. So there we were. Homeless.

It's true I don't remember much. And I don't think often about what I do remember.

And now here we are all over again. We never escaped.

The new town, Mom's jobs, my college applications—all part of a sick joke. They made us think we could get out of the trap of being poor. Fooled us into thinking we weren't drowning before the current dragged us back down.

Happy New Year, I think.

* * *

I try to help with the search, but there's nothing in our price range. And Mom doesn't seem to want my help. Earlier she wanted me to grow up and take responsibility. Now she just wants me to stay out of her way.

She gets Mr. Harrison to put off the repairs by three more days. But that just means three more days of stress. Of not knowing where I'll be sleeping at the end of it. I throw up in the bathroom at school every one of those days. Maybe it's just the morning sickness. It's coming more often now.

This time, I tell my friends right away. Madi asks her parents if I can stay over for a few weeks if need be. They say yes. As long as my mom gives permission.

I should be happy. "But what about Mom?"

Madi looks torn. "You know how my parents are. I really had to talk them into it. If your mom was coming too, they'd just back out." She shifts from foot to foot, uneasy. "I just don't want you and the bean to end up somewhere unsafe."

I can't expect the Wendts to let my whole family move in. It just bugs me how Madi's parents can be so selfish when they have so much. There are people with nothing who'll still give you the shirt off their back if you need it. But Madi's parents? They're the kind of rich people who'll think a long time and then *maybe* give you something old from their closet.

Mom still lights up when I tell her. Like this is the best news she's had all week. It probably is. She says a friend from work has offered to let her stay with her. But her apartment is in another suburb, far away from my school. By staying with Madi, I can keep up with my classes.

"You need to graduate," Mom says. "You can't let anything stop you."

So that's how I get dropped off at Madi's house, with my life in a battered backpack and Mom's suitcase. Mom took her stuff to her friend's house in trash bags.

But I need to make a good impression.

CHAPTER 12

Standing on the doorstep of Madi's house shouldn't feel like entering a villain's lair. I've been here a million times. But this feels different. Mom's car pulls away, leaving me alone. She called and worked out all the details ahead of time. And while Madi's parents aren't the greatest, they aren't evil. I should not feel like Prince Ivan from *The Firebird*, facing down Koschei the Deathless. I should ring the doorbell and stop being dramatic. It's winter. I need to go in and thaw myself out.

Instead, I hesitate. Frozen on the doorstep. Holding my right glove in my left hand.

It would be easier not to worry if life weren't so dramatic now. When senior year started, I'd have laughed if someone had told me I'd be pregnant and homeless before graduation. And it's not like I have nothing left to lose. I have Little Bean to worry about now. Sleeping or doing whatever fetuses do before they can kick. Peaceful, not even able to sense hunger or cold.

All this stress can't be good for it.

Maybe if I'd gone to Illinois, Mom and I wouldn't be homeless now. But you know what? After she got over the first shock, Mom stopped lashing out. She bent over backward to be nice to me and not snap from stress. She kept saying the landlord would have tried to kick us out anyway. He was just looking for an excuse to find new tenants and raise the rent even higher. That was the last thing she said as we packed.

I still feel like it's my fault. Like it's a punishment for thinking I could be a mom. For imagining I was grown-up enough, strong enough, good enough to take care of a kid.

The fingers of my right hand are getting numb. It's time to ring the bell.

* * *

Madi opens the door. Before I can put down my backpack, she leads me over to her parents. They're sitting at the kitchen table, rather than in the formal living room. But

I still feel nervous. Chrome appliances gleam. The kitchen counters are made of bright green stone. Not a chip in sight. This is a perfect room. My worn-out purple backpack, bought secondhand and used since freshman year, sticks out. I stick out.

They don't know I'm pregnant. Madi hid it from them. If I stay here too long, they'll find out. Does it matter? They've never been comfortable with my family. My mom is almost twenty years younger than them and a whole lot poorer. It makes them nervous. They make me nervous.

"Ashley can stay here for the next two weeks," Madi's dad says to her. "Did you set up the guest room already?"

He doesn't even look at me.

I say, "Hi, Mr. Wendt. Thank you for letting me stay over. I really appreciate it."

He smiles at me as if noticing me for the first time. Mrs. Wendt gives me a hug and says she hopes we can find a place soon. I worry she means so that I can leave. But then she goes off on our landlord. She's mad at him too. Madi's parents are not bad people. They really aren't.

I'm just so tired.

* * *

We put my stuff in the guest room. Change out the fancy bedspread for a warm winter comforter. Madi sits down on the bed with a thump.

"Jasleen invited me over today. She wants to watch this new K-drama together. It sounds like something you'd like."

"I think I'm going to unpack and rest," I say.

Like I'm someone who drove for hours to get here. It's just the other side of town. The show sounds good, and I do want to see Jasleen. I used to see her outside school more. When I was a regular at the dance group. Back in October, dance seemed so important. Danny and I broke up over it.

Danny. I should tell him. I should do a lot of things.

It's just . . . right now, I want to sleep more than I want anything else.

"Okay," says Madi. "I can stay with you if you need."

"No, go. Say hi to Jasleen for me. I'll be fine. I need a nap. I get tired more now." It's true. The fetus sucks up more energy than such a tiny little thing could use. I guess it takes a lot just to grow.

I didn't mind that last week. I thought it was cool.

"If you're sure," Madi says, looking doubtful. She's worried about me. That makes me feel worse.

"I need to crash," I say. "Go. It'll be fun." I remember when I used to borrow Madi's fantasy books. When I used to read, and dance, and do fun things. Before my life became so grown-up. So hassled. So much like my mom's.

Madi goes. I change and curl up under the covers. The warmth brings no comfort. I'm exhausted, but I can't sleep. I feel all wrong. Little Bean presses on my bladder.

In Madi's bathroom, I see myself in the mirror over the sink. My face is breaking out. Hormones or stress or both. My eyes look dead. Like an escaped prisoner's or a shell-shocked soldier's.

Thinking of soldiers and PTSD reminds me. Last time I was here, I slept like a rock, thanks to Madi's Xanax. I didn't like it. It made me all groggy. But I slept.

Before I think about it, I'm opening the mirror door. Going through her medicine cabinet. Checking the names on the bottles of meds.

There it is.

Hating myself, I unscrew the childproof cap.

CHAPTER 13

Madi comes to check on me before breakfast. She doesn't notice anything. I nod along as she tells me about last night.

"The show was great. I wish you could have come. Jasleen was right, you'd totally love it. I just hope you were okay when I was out. I felt bad leaving you alone like that. I know you said it was fine, but you know you can tell me if it's not, right?"

I try to act normal. Like I didn't just steal her meds. She let me stay at her house. She convinced her parents. And here I am sneaking around like an addict.

Worse, maybe. It doesn't feel like I have a medical problem. The people at treatment centers are trying to get their bodies and minds to stop desperately craving drugs. But I didn't feel some terrible withdrawal. I'm not so hooked I can't stop. They say addiction is an illness, but I don't feel ill.

What scares me most is that I did it on impulse. Even I can't explain why. And because I can't explain it, I don't know if I'll do it again.

Don't I care enough about Little Bean—or myself—to stop? Life is hard enough already. Why am I making things worse?

I don't have a good answer.

"Ashley? Ashley?"

"Uh . . . sorry. I'm . . ."

She frowns in concern. "Wow, looks like you needed the sleep. I'll go make some oatmeal."

I go to the bathroom to brush my teeth. Splash cold water on my face. I don't look in the mirror this time. I don't want to see what's in it. And I know what lies behind it.

* * *

School is falling lower and lower on the list of things I care about. I'm even behind in Spanish now. Señora Díaz asks if I'm okay.

"This isn't like you."

But maybe this *is* me. This person who can't cope. Who

thought she was ready to take on the world, and now just wants to hide from it.

I do my best to put her off and arrive at math class just in time for the bell. Stare at the triangles on the board and try to look like I'm paying attention. There's no point in pretending. My life is already falling apart just because the landlord found out. But eventually *everyone* will see it. What a fraud I am.

My belly will pop out, and the rumors will start. I don't think I can take it. The staring, the way they'll label me. So many people in this town expect life to be picture-perfect. They like it the way it is. White, suburban, and rich. *Classy*, they call it. They resent you if you ruin the picture.

At lunch, I finally look at my phone. A missed call from Mom last night. Plus, a text checking in.

How are you doing?

I lie. Stick on a fake emoji smile.

All good. ☺ *You?*

I force myself to eat something.

Jasleen pulls up next to me as we leave the cafeteria. "Ashley?"

I turn to see what she wants and feel the telltale signs of nausea. Mouth clamped shut, I run. Jasleen follows. The bathroom is busy. No stalls open. Gossip runs down the short line.

"Let Ashley through! Looks like she's going to hurl!"

"Isn't she the one who got so sick after one beer, she thought she had Covid?"

I'm too sick to care. Or to tell them it was two. They let me cut the line. I make for the next empty stall. Jasleen stands outside the shut door and asks if I'm okay. I don't know where to start.

"Let me take you to the nurse's office," she says when I come out. I can't say that I'm not sick in front of the others. So I go along with it.

"What do you think the nurse can do?" I mutter.

"Let you lie down for an hour," Jasleen shoots back. Which is hard to argue with. "You're not weak if you need a rest after everything you've gone through. Between you-know-what and basically being evicted."

"I feel weak." The words come out before I can stop them. Jasleen doesn't know how weak I am. She doesn't even know about the first time I took Xanax. Let alone yesterday.

"Yeah, that's what my cousin Rajinder said." Jasleen stops in the hall. We're only halfway to the nurse's office. "He isn't weak, and you aren't either."

She's only mentioned her cousin once before. "Is he the one who was there during the Oak Creek shooting?"

Jasleen is Sikh. About ten years ago, a racist went on a gun rampage against the Sikh community in Oak Creek. When I met Jasleen in freshman year, I didn't want her to know the only reason I'd heard of her religion was because of the mass shooting. But she brought it up once. Her second cousin had just come to this country, and he was right there when it happened. Her parents helped him after.

"Yeah," Jasleen says. "He lost his job two years later. He

was arguing with everyone and breaking down at work. He was scared of losing his visa because of getting fired. My dad found Rajinder a new job. He came to live with us for a while. My mom pushed him to go to therapy for his PTSD. He sounded just like you. *I feel weak. I'm alive, so why am I complaining?*" Jasleen makes a sound halfway between sympathy and a snort.

"I wasn't in a mass shooting. I didn't see anyone die. I just need to pull myself together."

Jasleen stares at me. "That wasn't the point! I didn't tell you his story so that you could feel even worse about yourself."

"Then what was the point?" It comes out sharper than I mean it to.

"The point is that it's not weak to need help. Nobody can go it alone, Ashley! I know your mom had to because her parents were like that. But you don't have to be some kind of stoic superhero. You're human. And you've been through a lot. It's okay to get help for what you're feeling. My cousin ended up wishing he'd done it years ago."

I want to say something bitter. Does she think I'm as rich as Madi, to have a therapist and meds? People like me, we just keep going.

But I'm *not* going. I'm drowning. Jasleen's right. It's not weak to reach out.

CHAPTER 14

Who can help me?

No one if I don't tell. I can't tell Mom. The thought of saying the words to her shuts me down. There's just no way. I scroll past her number on my phone.

My friends can't help. Madi would feel bad about the first pill, the one she gave me. And I'm staying at her house. I trust her, but I can't risk the roof over my head. Jasleen gave me a hint. But what if she tells Madi? She's already burdened by keeping my secret from Danny.

I browse through my contacts and find a new number. It's for Dr. Erickson's office. From when I had the appointment. The one where the ultrasound tech showed me Little Bean.

Even if everything's falling apart, I can't give up. I chose to have this baby. I said I'd be strong enough for it. That means asking for help. No matter how scared I am.

A doctor will know what to do. And she has to protect my privacy. She'll be able to tell me what's wrong. How to stop. How to be the mom I used to believe I could be.

I call and ask when I can come in.

*　*　*

It's harder to get there now. I have to ask Madi to drive me. She has to lie to her parents. If they knew I was going to the doctor, they would worry. If they knew what kind of doctor . . .

I also have to lie to Madi. I tell her I'm getting a blood test. Routine. Nothing to worry about. I hate how easily she believes me. But I'm her best friend. What reason would I have to lie?

She drops me off. Says she'll pick me up in an hour. She'll drive around till then. I almost say something about wasting gas. I don't. She doesn't need to save money.

I go in alone.

I didn't say over the phone why I needed to come in. I just said I was worried. They asked if I was bleeding. I said no. They seemed relaxed. But I got an appointment quickly.

I barely have to wait.

Then I'm in the exam room. And I remember how Dr. Erickson was last time. Judging me for not starting folic acid sooner. I almost chicken out.

There's no point in being scared. I need her help. I'm not going to let a frown scare me. Or a memory.

I tell her everything. Almost. I say "a friend" instead of Madi's name. I don't want to get her in trouble over the first pill. But Dr. Erickson's eyebrows shoot way up when she hears I'm living with that friend now.

"You need to stop," she says. "For your baby's sake."

I bite my tongue. *Yeah, duh. That's why I'm telling you.* At the same time, panic wells up. What if Little Bean doesn't make it because of something I've done? How could I live with myself?

"How?" I ask. "Can you help me?"

Dr. Erickson sighs. Then she catches herself. Like she knows she's not supposed to do that but can't help it.

"There's a rehab place that's good with pregnant women. I'll give them a call. They're in Appleton."

That's hours away. With good traffic. It doesn't sound practical.

"That's . . ." I don't know what the word is. "Would I have to live there?"

"It's residential," Dr. Erickson says blandly.

"I have school. My mom is here. I can't . . . I mean, could I get counseling or something? And stay here?"

"You're not living with your mother," the doctor points out. "Your living situation gives you access to drugs. I don't recommend outpatient. You need to be living on site."

This is moving way too fast. Like a rip current at the beach when we lived in Milwaukee. I don't have time to think.

I thrash, trying to keep from drowning.

"Can we do something where I can stay in school? It's not like I'm getting high all the time. It only happened twice. And I've been really stressed out. I need some help with that."

Dr. Erickson stares at me. "I'm glad you told me. But you need to take the help you're being offered. Not play down how serious this is. Going to Appleton is the best thing you can do for your baby."

My hand goes to my stomach. It's instinct. To shield it. But I can't protect Little Bean from myself.

"How long would I be there?" I ask.

"It depends on how your recovery goes. But you know it would be the right thing. Think of your child. It deserves the best start."

"I'll think about it," I promise. "Do you know a counselor who takes BadgerCare? Around here, I mean. Does the rehab place take my plan?"

"Your plan covers the services but not room and board."

Well, that's it then. I'm not going somewhere I'd have to pay who knows what, for who knows how long. There's got to be a better way.

"I don't think it's a good idea. I mean—" I try to think of a good way to say this. One that won't make her judge me more. "It's the stress. It's getting to me. I think that's the real problem. When we lost our apartment—"

"Exactly," she says. "You need a place to stay."

She doesn't get it at all. She's not listening. I shut down and get through the rest of the appointment. It's earlier than she expected me, but not so early she can't run the blood test. The one that will say if the baby has Down syndrome. At my age, she says, Down is very unlikely. But the same test can tell me what sex Little Bean will be when they're born.

I wish I could feel excited about finding that out. Instead, I feel like I shouldn't have come. Like I reached out only to get slapped back.

CHAPTER 15

The weird thing is, in some ways it does help. Saying the truth out loud. Naming the problem. Asking the question. Even if I didn't get an answer I could use.

Dr. Erickson wasn't wrong about living in Madi's house. The temptation of it. But I can't afford what she offered me instead. So I have to make myself be able to live here. Safely. *Without* taking pills from Madi's cabinet when things get to be too much.

I didn't do this kind of thing before, when I felt like I had some control. But taking the Xanax doesn't make me feel in control. It helps in the moment. Then it makes things worse.

Anyway, I can't get my old life back. It's time to move forward.

I figure it won't be enough to promise myself not to take the pills again. I'll just do it again next time everything gets unbearable. I think about something Madi learned in therapy, about distraction. When she wanted to self-harm, she'd put her earbuds in instead. Listen to a long song, about seven minutes long, then another. It didn't always work. But it helped, she told me later. And eventually, she didn't have to distract herself much at all.

I figure I'll try that. I bookmark a long ballet clip on YouTube.

And over the next few days, things start getting better. Even things I don't control. Mom calls me all excited. She's signing a lease for a new place. It's in the same school district. We can move in next month. It's not my fault about the old one, she tells me. It's been scary, but we'll be better off with a different landlord. We'll be back together soon. As a family.

The doctors' office sends a social worker to the Wendts' house to convince me to go to rehab. Madi's parents are out grocery shopping when she comes. I tell the social worker that I can't let her in because this isn't my house. We talk on the doorstep instead. I say I really, really can't go to Appleton. The winter cold drives her off before the Wendts get back.

There's other great news. Little Bean's blood test results look good. And he's going to be a boy! I take a screenshot to send to my mom. Her grandson. Madi gives me a high five, and it wipes out Mr. Harrison's lying congratulations. I have people who care about me. Who're rooting for me and the baby. I can do this.

I can even tell Danny. The thought doesn't scare me now. It helps that the morning sickness is fading away. I don't feel like throwing up anymore. That alone is a big relief.

I plan to text Danny tonight. It will go better in writing. Even though we broke up, I trust him to care about the kid.

***

I write the message with the "send to" section blank. I don't want to accidentally text him halfway through a sentence. Or before reading it over.

Someone knocks on the door of the guest room. It's not Madi. The pattern of knocking is different.

I open the door and see her mother, who looks stunned. Disappointed.

"Ashley, the police are here for you," she says.

I freeze. Are they going to arrest me? Madi said giving anyone else her meds was illegal. Is she going to jail too? And how could they know about it? I thought doctors couldn't tell anyone. How badly have I messed up?

I don't want to go to jail, I think stupidly. *I don't.*

I follow Mrs. Wendt downstairs. She doesn't say a word.

There are two cops in the hall. A man and a woman, both young. Madi is there too. She stands by the open door in shock. Her mother closes it against the cold wind. Then she stands by her daughter.

I'm alone.

"Ashley Muller?" says the young female officer.

I nod. That's my name. For some reason, all I remember in that moment is that I wanted it changed to *Hoffman*.

"We're here to take you into custody under Act 292, the Unborn Child Protection Act."

Mrs. Wendt makes a sound. She didn't know I was pregnant.

This has to be a mistake. The name of the law sounds fake. But these people look like real cops. And the Wendts won't let me stay here after this. Even if it's all a mistake.

"What do you mean? Ma'am," I add. These are police. I have to be polite. And careful. "I'm being arrested?"

"No," the male officer cuts in after his partner hesitates. "This is not a criminal arrest. It's about child neglect. We're taking you into custody till your hearing in juvenile court, which will be tomorrow. Please cooperate with us."

Child neglect. I remember back to Milwaukee. How Child Protective Services would take kids away because someone reported the parents. Even if the report was wrong, the court didn't always give the kids back. Especially if the parents were homeless. We'd been homeless during the divorce too. Much later, when we were back on our feet, Mom told me how scared she'd been of losing me to the system.

That sort of thing didn't seem to happen here. In this town where everything looked perfect on the surface.

"There's a mistake," I say. "I'm eighteen. Yes, we got evicted, and I'm couch surfing right now. But you don't need to put me in foster care. I'm an adult."

"The child being neglected isn't you. It's your unborn baby. There's an allegation of drug use against you. Your doctor says you're refusing services. We're empowered to take you into custody to protect the unborn child. Please come with us."

Wait, what? They want to take me so they can protect Little Bean . . . from me? Where are they taking me? And what do they mean, I'm not being arrested?

Then Madi screams, a wounded animal sound. She breaks away from her mother.

"I'm so sorry. This is all my fault. I gave the pill to her. I didn't mean to hurt anybody. She was scared and freaking out, and I thought it would help. Please don't arrest her. She's a good person. This is all my fault!"

The cops talk right over her, telling Mrs. Wendt to make

sure Madi doesn't interfere. They don't seem to care she confessed. They're focused on getting me to come with them.

Mrs. Wendt is almost as pale with fear as her daughter. She tries to guide Madi away gently. There's no amount of rich that makes you not scared when the cops are in your house.

I don't want anyone getting hurt. I know Madi's probably having a panic attack. The police don't know.

"It's okay," I tell her. "I'll go talk to them. They said they're not arresting me. Nobody . . . nobody freak out, okay?"

The last part is to myself as much as to her. This can't be happening. It's too unreal. A dream. A nightmare.

CHAPTER 16

The cops say they're not taking me to jail. They tell me to pack my clothes and a toothbrush. I stuff everything into my backpack. I don't have time to pack the suitcase.

The police put me in the back of their car. We drive past the station. Out of the suburbs, and into the biggest city in the county. They explain that they're driving me to the county juvenile shelter home. They tacked "home" on to make it sound nicer. It's where they keep teenagers waiting for their court dates for minor crimes. I don't remind them that I'm eighteen. I don't want them to take me somewhere worse.

The shelter doesn't look like a jail. There are trees on the lawn and no gates. It still terrifies me.

"What happens if I don't go in?" I ask.

It's a stupid question. I have no way to get home from here. No home to go back to. I'd be wandering the streets in the middle of January. Trying to get to where my mom's staying.

Mom. I need to tell her where I am. She'll be so worried.

"If you run away from here, you'll be taken to jail until your hearing tomorrow," one of the cops says.

Okay. There's going to be a . . . hearing? Trial? Some kind of court thing. And it's soon. I'll be able to explain myself. I wasn't "refusing services." I asked for help. I told the doctor everything. I just didn't want to go to a place that's far away and costs money I don't have. It's not what it looks like.

I'd better go along quietly now, so they believe me in court tomorrow.

I go inside. As the staff process my details, I see why it's called a shelter. Not because it's a place where people help you, but because it's an institution. Like a homeless shelter. A place where rules matter and people don't.

Someone official goes through my backpack. She confiscates my deodorant because it's a spray can. My razor goes too, of course. That one I understand. But losing the deodorant makes me feel lousy. Low. I hope they give me something before I go to court. I imagine the judge's nose turning up at me and my lack of grooming. My clothes are taken to get sanitized in the dryer. The staffer doesn't want bedbugs.

The staff member also takes my prenatal vitamins. She can't tell what's in them. There's a form I'll have to fill out about medical conditions. A doctor will see me soon. I don't know when soon is.

Dr. Erickson was so upset I hadn't started the vitamins earlier. Now her report has landed me in a place where I can't have them. I don't argue with the staffer. I know the vitamins are important. But everything is too strange. I have to save my strength for the hearing. To get out of here.

The lady keeps going through my stuff. When she finds my computer, she gets angry. Not with me though. She asks who told me I could bring a computer. It could get stolen. She's not responsible for people bringing large electronics here. Someone should have told me not to pack it.

I don't know what to say. Was I supposed to leave it at Madi's house? No one told me much of anything about where I was going.

I just sit there and let everything wash over me.

No point in trying anymore.

At least I'm allowed to call my mom now.

I call her on the youth shelter's phone—the lady took my cell phone. The call goes to voicemail. I bet Mom didn't pick up because it was an unknown number.

When the voicemail beeps, I start trying to explain. I don't know if I'm making sense. I start crying. I don't hang up until the machine cuts me off. The big sobs don't stop.

I didn't want to tell my mom what I'd done before this. But now I just want to hear a familiar voice, even if she's mad at me. I just want someone to tell me it will be all right.

The kitchen was closed by the time we got here. I hadn't eaten at Madi's house yet. When I stop crying enough to say

I'm hungry, the staff give me a pathetic little snack. I didn't used to get hungry. Little Bean needs to grow though.

Maybe they'd give me more if I asked. But I'm afraid to ask now. I need to keep my head down till tomorrow. It's not like asking anyone for anything has done me any good.

Eventually they leave me alone in a room. No roommate, which is good. I can't talk to any more strangers. Worn out, I collapse onto the bed without changing my clothes. And then I lie there. Tired, bloated, and queasy. Even though I've eaten almost nothing.

Sleep does not come. It's worse than the first night at Madi's house. Worse than anything I've ever felt.

If I had the Xanax now, I'd take it, I think. *I'd take the whole bottle. I'd rather be dead than feel like this.*

What about Little Bean? Fear passes through me like a wave. Violent. Overwhelming.

I cup my hand over the slight curve. So small it could be mistaken for gaining weight. So fragile.

"I'm so sorry," I say out loud. "I love you. I would never hurt you."

What if I already have? Everything I've done has only made things worse. From the very first day I knew I was pregnant.

"You're going to be okay," I tell my baby. Because that's what moms say.

But even I don't believe me.

CHAPTER 17

A staffer wakes me up the next morning. My court hearing is in two hours. I scramble to get ready. Wash the crust off my eyelids. Brush my hair till every snag is gone. I have breakfast, even though I'm afraid of throwing up in court. The morning sickness is mostly gone, but who knows?

Still. I can't be faint with hunger either. This is my one chance. I have to make a good impression.

I can get out of here. I just need to explain.

So I try to smile at everyone. To be friendly. To hide that inside, I'm terrified.

The police come again. They transport me to the courtroom.

My case will be up first. It's called *In the interest of Baby Boy Muller*. I am not giving Little Bean that last name. If the police had shown up at Madi's ten minutes later, Danny Morales would know about the kid. It may be hard to think about Danny. The first guy I loved. The first guy I *stopped* loving. But I know he wouldn't abandon his own child. I know from the way he takes care of his siblings.

As soon as I get out of here, I'll tell him. I try not to think about how he'd look at me if he knew about the drugs.

It's time.

They call me into the courtroom. People introduce themselves. There's the commissioner, who is like a judge. But not really a judge. And the corporation counsel. Who is like the DA. A prosecutor. But also not really. They say he's for cases that aren't criminal.

"Wait," I say. "If it's not criminal, why did they arrest me? And who is my lawyer?"

I have a right to a lawyer, don't I? Jasleen always said, if you get arrested at a protest, don't say anything. They'll twist it. Keep quiet and ask for a lawyer. I don't think she ever thought about getting arrested for a crime.

But they said this wasn't a crime. Nothing makes sense.

The commissioner says, "We wanted to get you a lawyer as soon as possible. But the usual person for these Act 292 cases had a medical emergency last week. We're trying to find someone to take your case before the next hearing."

I'm still confused.

"Next hearing? When is that?" *What* is that, I want to ask.

"It will be less than thirty days from now," he says impatiently. "This is an initial custody hearing. You'll get a chance to speak at the end of it."

He hurries the hearing along, and I fall silent. I don't want to make him angry. Not when I'll be seeing him again in a few weeks.

The first person to talk is the social worker. The one who came to the Wendts' house. She paints a picture of me not letting her in. Leaving her standing in the winter cold. Refusing her help. Saying I couldn't talk to her. Shooing her off.

She paints a picture of *me*.

I'm homeless, she tells the court about me. In an unstable situation. According to Dr. Erickson's notes, I said someone I was living with gave me drugs. I'm in school, but I'm not living with my parents. They're divorced. I have an absent father and a mother who struggles to provide what I need. I'm an adult, but not a responsible one. I had an unplanned pregnancy in high school. I was sarcastic when my doctor told me about the risks of not taking folic acid. I knowingly took drugs while pregnant. On multiple occasions. I revealed this to Dr. Erickson. But I didn't seem to understand how serious it was. Or how it could affect my unborn child. I refused her offers of help. I made excuses to avoid rehab. I didn't realize this could be life or death for the baby. Dr. Erickson reported me because she was worried for the child's welfare. I needed to be stopped from using drugs again.

This is how she paints me. I'm a neglectful mother. Just as if I had given a toddler the Xanax.

The social worker recommends I be kept in the youth shelter for now.

She doesn't like to advise this when I am so young. She doesn't like to keep expectant mothers in custody. The commissioner knows she usually tries to keep them at home, with family. But since I am already homeless, says the social worker, this is better for both me and the unborn child. The youth shelter will give me stability. Remove me from bad influences. Keep me away from drugs.

To hear her talk about me, you wouldn't know we barely spoke for five minutes. That I sent her away because the Wendts would be back from grocery shopping soon. That I was hiding the pregnancy because this is how people would see me. Like the social worker does. In a fun-house mirror.

Every bad choice I have made is huge. Blown up. Everything I've done *right* becomes tiny, and then vanishes. I'm not someone who fights for my baby. Not in this mirror. I'm just someone he needs protecting from.

This is how I look to the world. This is how I'll always look. Everyone's worst idea of a teen mom. Irresponsible. Careless. A girl everyone can look down on.

The worst part is that even I look down on me. Because nothing the social worker said was a lie.

CHAPTER 18

I don't even listen to the corporation counsel. I just sit there, all the fight gone out of me. Maybe they're right about me. Little Bean deserves a mom who's more mature. Someone who can take care of him. It's too bad he's stuck with me.

Even my name for him is childish. He's not a bean sprout growing in a plastic bag. A little kid's science experiment. Something that won't matter a month later. I really do sound like a child who doesn't get it.

Besides, even that bean in a bag was too much for me. My plant never sprouted. I couldn't take care of it right. I should be listening now, and I can't focus. I can't do anything. Not anything that matters. I used to be proud of my good grades in AP Spanish. My Borges presentation. Proud that I was going to go to college, like my parents never got to.

It's all meaningless now. I was proud of what I could do while someone else took care of me. While Mom kept a roof over my head. Made sure I had everything I needed for school. Paid for my health care, even when she had none.

What made me think I could be a rock like that for my baby? When I still need that support myself?

The counsel sits down. I'm not sure what he said. I need to know what they're saying. I can't zone out now.

The problem is, this is not much like what I thought a court would be. On TV shows, witnesses answer questions from the two sides' lawyers. This is very different. Each person gives a short speech. No one asks questions. And there is no lawyer for my side. I don't know what I'll say when I get a chance. Whether anything I say will mean anything.

The next person to talk is a man in his thirties. He introduces himself as the GAL. Guardian ad litem, he explains to me. A type of lawyer.

"Representing the interest of the Baby Boy Muller."

I remember telling my friends I was going to have a

baby, and thinking about how I didn't want to give it my dad's name. Muller, the name of the father who doesn't bother to call. The court doesn't know that. But they've decided that's who Little Bean is going to be. Before he's even born.

I don't know who Baby Boy Muller is. Neither does this stranger. Who is he? What does he know about any of this?

"Looking at Dr. Erickson's notes, I think it would be against the best interests of the unborn child to release the mother from custody right now. She needs to be under supervision. To prevent further neglect in the form of illegal drug use at this critical time."

Under all the fancy lawyer talk, the meaning is clear. He doesn't want to let me go because he thinks I might use drugs again.

Anger and helplessness and shame all wash over me.

Anger at all these people who don't know me. Who don't care about me. Who don't care about the baby. No matter what they say. They didn't even know I was pregnant till I was reported. Where were they when my mom and

I got kicked out? Did they care about my baby then? Or did they only start to care when they got a chance to judge?

And I feel helpless because it doesn't matter. Nothing I do matters. All my vows to stop drifting. To take control of my life. They mean nothing. I'm more trapped than I've ever been. I hate Jasleen suddenly. She told me to get help. To be brave in reaching out. And it put me here.

Underneath it all, the shame. Because I did take those pills. The second time without anyone offering. The second time knowing it was bad for the baby. In that moment, I did not care. The next day I was so upset with myself. But when I did it, I only cared about shutting it all off. Shutting myself off. Stopping the fear I felt. The loneliness.

The anger and the helplessness.

I want to scream that these people are making it worse. Last night was the worst I've ever felt. But what if they're right? What if they know better? What if I just need to let the grown-ups do their jobs?

The social worker with her training.

The slick GAL with his law school degree. Now he's

saying that when the baby is born, they'll need to consider if I can keep it. If I'm able to care for *Baby Boy Muller* as he needs.

My hands curl around my stomach, as if they could take Little Bean right now.

I look at them all. I was never this afraid of anyone. Not Mr. Harrison when he lied so smoothly. Not Dr. Erickson when I didn't know what she could do.

They have my child's future in their hands. They could take him from me in the hospital. Put him in the system. With one little paper, they could make me no longer a mom.

Of course I'm scared of them. That fun-house mirror me, the only me they know . . .

That is how they will decide my baby is better off without me.

CHAPTER 19

Nothing prepares you for this. No class presentation, no dance performance. Nothing makes you ready to argue for your freedom and your family. You never think of freedom as something you'll lose.

It's like something out of *The Firebird*. As if I'm stuck in Koschei's castle. Trapped, till Prince Ivan and the Firebird come to save all his prisoners.

But there are no heroes here.

I should have made notes, I think. *Last night. I should have gotten ready.* Then I remember they took my computer and my phone. And I didn't know how the hearing would go. I thought I'd have someone to argue for me.

Mom would scream if she knew the fetus inside me has a lawyer and I don't.

No. Don't think about Mom. How she's not here. Don't think about how alone you are.

Baby Boy Muller has a lawyer. But Baby Boy Muller doesn't exist. Little Bean only has me. I might be a failure. I might be a mess. But I am all he has right now.

I'm not sure I can fight for myself. I used to have dreams. Studying languages. Joining a dance troupe at college. Now those feel as unrealistic as being a star in the Paris Ballet. My body knows it hasn't danced in months.

My dreams keep shrinking down. Lately they've just been the basics. Having a roof over my head. Staying in school. Getting to doctor's appointments. Not taking the pills again.

Now they're not even that. The only thing I want now is to escape this. Like I'm an animal in a trap. And I don't even have that drive, that urge to live. The thing that makes even a raccoon chew its leg off to get free.

I'm tired. I'm done.

They can say I'm a bad person. An unfit mom. Someone who can't be trusted. I don't know how to prove them wrong. They'll all believe each other first. Before they believe me.

There's only one thing left that can get me back on my feet. I can't give up on Little Bean. I never could. The day I decided I wasn't going to get an abortion, I knew it. I had to try. I still do. If I don't, I will always look back and wonder. I will always think maybe I could have been a good parent. Not to some future kid with some future guy. To this one now.

I knew then what I know now. The only thing that could ever make me give up on him is believing what everyone says about me. And *that* would be failing Little Bean. I can't let what other people think of me matter more to me than he does.

But even if I do my best, I know it's useless. I've been judged already.

So what. *So what?* I have to try.

* * *

When the GAL is done, the commissioner turns to me.

"Ms. Muller? Do you have a position on whether or how the baby and you should be held in custody?"

It's my turn to talk, but will they listen?

"I think I should be sent to stay with my mother. She just signed a lease. We're not going to be homeless anymore," I say. I don't add that we can't move in till next month. We'll figure something out. "I think if I could be with my family, it would feel safer. For me and my baby. Better than the youth shelter."

Safer. That's something they'll listen to. And it's true. But I don't mean safe from the troubled teens at the shelter. I mean safe from *them*.

The commissioner looks curious. "What's the address you would be living at with your mom? That could be a good option here. More stable."

"I don't know." It all falls apart.

"You mean you don't know where you would live?"

"It's in the same school district. I didn't see the new lease," I say. I know that's not enough. "I feel so bad in that shelter. I wish I could go home."

The commissioner brings his hands together, fingertips touching. He peers over his hands at me. "Look. I can't send you to an uncertain living situation. At the youth shelter, we'll know where you are. You'll have a court date in a few weeks. It's better than being in jail."

"In jail!" I don't mean to say anything. It just comes out, like an echo. From the emptiness inside me.

"Because you're young and still in school, I want you to be able to keep studying. The shelter has a school program. I've seen women as young as you kept in the county jail waiting for their next hearing. I'd like to avoid that."

The rules don't make sense. They keep saying this isn't a criminal trial. That I'm not charged with a crime. That this is a child welfare case.

But I was hauled off by police. And now they say they can put me in jail.

I can't get a grip on this thing. On what's possible. What's not. It all slips out of my grasp.

And then it's over. They're taking me back to the youth shelter. The next hearing is in twenty-five days. The next hearing on where I'm going to be stuck and for how long. The next hearing *In the interest of Baby Boy Muller*.

CHAPTER 20

They drive me back to the shelter. I'm numb, but I know I should be panicking. I'm trapped, and nobody knows where I am. I don't know if I made enough sense on the phone for Mom to find me. What if I'm lost in the system? Forgotten?

"Did my mom call back?" I ask. I'm almost afraid of the answer. I don't believe she'd ever abandon me, but the hearing shook me. The girl they described there is a person no one wants for a daughter.

A staffer named Tasha explains that incoming calls go to a different number than the outgoing ones. I need to send my mom the right number for her to call me back. That information got lost in the chaos last night.

So maybe Mom's been trying to call me back all day and not getting through. I need to get her that number. I can't get through this alone.

The staff give me back my phone so I can text my mom the shelter phone number. They also let me copy a few numbers out of my contacts. I write them down on a piece of paper.

Then they take my cell phone away again. I can make calls on the landline. Short ones. Others might be waiting to use the phone.

The rules the staff explain are unending. No going out without permission. I can earn the privilege. With points. By doing chores. It's like one of Danny's video games, except everything is horrible. It's real life, and I can't just quit.

No letting anyone in my room. No going in anyone else's room. No hanging out in a whole list of places. No gang signs. No helping anyone else do their hair. No shaking hands. No human touch. Period. Only close relatives are allowed to visit me.

They ask me to fill out a form about my medical care. Since I'm eighteen, I don't need a parent to sign off on it. I'll get an appointment with a doctor soon.

I remember something through the numbness.

"I need prenatal vitamins," I say. "With folic acid."

A long dithering. There's no nurse here. Let alone a doctor. Is this something they can sign off on? They go back and forth. Tasha argues for me.

In the end, it's a yes. But wait till tomorrow.

* * *

The staffers warn me that they might be asked to come to my hearing. How I behave here at the youth shelter will decide where I go next.

But I don't need to be told again how much power the staff have over my future.

I ask to call my mom right away, but there's a change of shift for the staff. Which means they lock everyone in. I'm stuck in the room I spent last night in. There's nothing to do but think about things I'd rather forget. Phrases from the court hearing that I want to erase from my memory. But I come back to them against my will. They're burned into my brain now.

***

After the shift change, I want to try calling my mom again. The staff have rotated, so I can't find Tasha. But another staffer says one girl is talking to her lawyer, so the outgoing phone is busy. Someone from the boys' floor is next in line, and then me.

"You should go hang out in the lounge on your floor. That's where the incoming phone will ring if your mom calls. I'll come and get you when the other phone is free."

Lounge. Like we're in a fancy hotel.

Distance learning is over for the day, and everyone on the girls' floor is in the lounge. I get to know my neighbors.

I'm the oldest. Everyone else is a minor. Nobody's younger than twelve. Everyone's new, since you can only stay here two months.

Also, everyone has a story. Nobody says it exactly. But this place is halfway between a jail and an orphanage. There are girls here who barely missed landing in juvie. There are girls who are between foster homes and need somewhere to sleep. For some of them, it's a bit of both.

Everyone's waiting for a hearing. Some court to decide their fate.

I start to make sense of who's who here. There's the other pregnant girl, the nonbinary teen, the girl with the complex braids, and the scary kid.

The other pregnant girl is only fourteen. She's more pregnant than me, and shy. I wonder why anyone thought putting her here was a good idea. Then I wonder who did this to her, and shiver. There's no rape exception in the abortion law.

The staff call this the girls' floor. But there's also a nonbinary fifteen-year-old. They introduce themself to me. Act all cool. Say their biggest problem here is the staff took away their hair products. They don't want anyone keeping anything with alcohol in their room.

"Like anyone could drink that toxic stuff. You'd go blind," they say. "That's not how I'd sneak a drink in here anyway."

At first, I find the way the nonbinary kid talks off-putting. The obvious front. The fake tough attitude. Then

I realize they're not doing it because they're immature. They're doing it to head off being bullied. I'm new, and they don't know me. They don't know whether I'd decide they're an easy target.

The scary thirteen-year-old glares at both of us. I don't want to judge her, after the boxes I've been put in at court. But her angry stare freaks me out.

The phone in the lounge rings. The girl with the elaborate braids picks up. I forget her name, but she is seventeen, Black, short, and the next oldest here after me. I wonder how she manages those braids. Nobody's allowed to help her here. It seems like the kind of complicated hairstyle that needs an extra pair of hands.

She yells, "New girl! It's for you."

And I forget everything.

It's my mom. At last.

I think about trying to stay calm and cool. Then I realize the others are giving me space. Privacy. As much as they can, at least. Which isn't much. They huddle around the TV on the other side of the room.

Everybody here is away from their family. For one reason or another.

I take the phone. In one way at least, I'm one of the lucky ones here.

"Ashley!" I haven't heard Mom this frantic since I got lost on a beach in Milwaukee. She thought I got swept into Lake Michigan. "What happened? I've been terrified all day. I tried calling you back after your voicemail, but I couldn't get through. Then I got a call from someone saying she's your social worker and that you're in this home in the city. The Wendts said you were arrested. Where are you? Are you safe?"

She doesn't ask, *What did you do?*

After the nightmare this morning, I've forgotten what that's like. Being cared about. Being seen as a real human being. And not through the fun-house mirror.

CHAPTER 21

Even when Mom hears the whole story, she still sees me. Her daughter. Not some worthless failure.

Me.

She promises to visit me as often as she's allowed. It's only twenty-five days till my next hearing. She'll come to support me at court too.

She does scream when I tell her about the GAL, the lawyer for Baby Boy Muller. And how I didn't have one. But when she gets over the shock, she's scared.

"You need a lawyer, Ashley. This isn't just about keeping you somewhere against your will. It's about what happens when the baby's born. They're not going to let you keep him without a fight."

"They said I would have a lawyer at the next hearing," I say. But I'm not sure I believe them.

"It's better to have your own lawyer. Not someone they

assign you. Are you allowed to make other calls? There are some lawyers who will do it for free. This is important."

"I know it is," I say, a little impatient. "But they took my computer and my phone. I don't know who to call. I can't even google stuff. Do you . . . can you find anyone? Please?"

The last lawyer Mom knew was her divorce lawyer. And that was years ago.

"I'll try," she says. But I get the feeling it's going to be hard. If she knew who to call, we wouldn't have ended up homeless so fast. Not when what Mr. Harrison did was illegal. Not when we knew he was a liar.

Even though she'll do everything she can for me, this might be something she can't do.

But Mom's right. It needs to be done if I want to fight back for Little Bean. There are still months to go before he's born.

It will be summer then. Winter will be long over. The sun always comes back again. It's people who are less certain. Who aren't promised happy endings.

I am not a princess trapped in Koschei's castle. If I wait

for a hero to wake me up, I will be waiting forever. And I don't have forever. My breasts are sore all the time now. My bras barely fit. The weeks are ticking by.

Little Bean won't stay little or inside me forever. We're running out of time.

* * *

The next day, I'm put in a room with the others to do some kind of distance learning. A teacher is there to supervise us. But there's not much one teacher can do with so many different grades. The math they give me is way too hard, and there's no Spanish at all. I don't think learning is the point.

But one thing the teacher can do is give me scrap paper. I ask for a bit more to take back to my room. And a pen, because we're not allowed our own pencil sharpeners. That rule I get. They have those tiny blades.

I sit in my room after "school" and make a list. I haven't handwritten anything longer than a shopping list in a while. But with no way to type, it's back to fifth-grade cursive.

At the top, I write in big letters:

THE FIREBIRD LIST.

I draw her in the corner. Not the bird made of flame. The dancer. The one who made me dream, all those years ago in the Milwaukee library. With her tutu and her red feather hairpiece. It doesn't sparkle in pen. I'm not good at drawing.

I have to stop focusing on what I'm *not* good at. It's time to get stuff done. Be my own mythic hero.

Underneath the dramatic title, I add: *(how to get a lawyer for my hearing).*

Just in case any staffer worries that "firebird" is code for arson or something. You never know.

I make bullet points.

- *People I know who might have heard of this law. Jasleen? She's always reading the news.*
- *Check if things work in real life like she says though.*

Then I stop. I cross that second line out. Jasleen didn't know what I needed help with when she told me to reach out for help. She saw I was struggling and needing someone to talk to. What I did with what she told me isn't her fault. Neither is what happened to me next. I'm not going to be petty.

Besides, I'm not sure how to check anything right now. Or if I'm even allowed to call Jasleen.

I add a new bullet point.

- *Get enough points to go to the library. Google lawyers there. Check reviews.*

But wouldn't that show me lawyers who want money? The ones who pay for ads?

I'm stuck.

There's a knock on my door. The girl with the braids is outside.

"New girl! Want to come watch *The Mandalorian*?"

I do. I didn't have Disney+, so I never saw it. Just heard everyone talking about Baby Yoda.

Although on second thought . . . maybe I don't want to watch a show about a guy on the run with a baby. I get the feeling Baby Yoda is in danger a lot.

"I have to work on this list," I say. "Sorry."

The girl's face falls. I don't want her to think I don't want to hang out.

"I'm Ashley," I say. "What's your name?"

"Cynthia," she says. "After my aunt."

"That's cool. I'm not after anybody. That I know of."

"What's your list?" Cynthia asks. "I don't think we have homework."

Everything in me that's been hurt warns, *Careful. Don't trust people. You don't know anyone else's story.*

Even a doctor didn't keep things private.

"It's kind of personal," I say. "But I'm not getting far on it. So I'll come watch the show."

Hugs and touch are banned here. But people are still people. They reach out. In whatever way they can.

* * *

I do have nightmares about being chased around the galaxy after that. Evil Giancarlo Esposito hunts for Little Bean. And then he corners us in that courtroom.

When I wake up, I can't remember what the baby

looked like in my dream. It was born. It must have had a name that wasn't a small plant.

I should start thinking about names. I like the name Francisco. But I think I should ask Danny before I give the kid a name from his culture. Maybe he doesn't want that. Or maybe he'd really like it, except it's the name of this one cousin he hates. Who knows? I don't, because I didn't get to tell him.

I wish again that the police had come ten minutes later. Then I wouldn't have to imagine what Danny thinks. I feel like when he finds out, I'll see what kind of dad he'll be. His reaction to the reality.

I could wait till I'm out of here to tell him. This is not a great way for him to find out. It doesn't look good on my part. I'm not going to come off as a responsible future parent. I'll have to tell him about the Xanax. Maybe I can put off telling him a little longer. Avoid hearing what he thinks of me now. Fantasies of picking baby names together are just that: fantasies.

And then I remember that the baby might not keep the

name I give him. Not because he'll want a different one when he grows up. But because I might not be allowed to raise him. Because CPS might take him away. His new parents might call him by another name.

At least if Danny is involved, maybe CPS will let Little Bean go live with his dad when he's born. If they decide I'm not good enough to keep him.

Next morning, I add one more thing to my list. No matter how scared I am, I'm telling Danny. He has to know. For Little Bean's sake.

CHAPTER 22

It's time to make the leap. Like a bird jumping out of its nest, I have to take a risk to fly.

Tasha is back on duty today. But no prenatal vitamins yet. I tell her my doctor told me it was important.

It's true. I'm nervous about not having them.

It's also a show. I'm doing all the things that will show I can be a good parent. And making sure they're noticed.

I'm being graded at the end of the twenty-five days, and I know it.

Tasha is really apologetic about the vitamins. They're allowed, but someone forgot to buy them. The staff can't give me the ones I brought in. I don't understand, but she's trying to help me.

Another thing the staff should see? Me actively co-parenting. Besides, it's not like I can tell Danny without going through them. They control the phone calls out.

He's not my social worker or my family. So I might not be allowed.

After the lack of vitamins, Tasha is glad she can do something after all.

"He counts as family," she says firmly. "How could we not let you call the father of your baby?"

I'm glad she doesn't say boyfriend or partner. Because he isn't either of those things. But she's right about family. By a weird twist of fate, Danny Morales is going to be part of my life for a long, long time.

It's not a connection I planned on. Maybe it would have been better for us to remember each other as high school sweethearts. A summer crush brewing over ice cream. The first time either of us really dated someone. The first breakup that really hurt.

In that world, I didn't get pregnant. I think about it for a while. It feels strange. How can I fight for Little Bean while also feeling sad now? Mourning a world I've lost. A world where the past few months never were. A world where he would never be.

But you know what? I'm allowed to feel sad. And stressed. And conflicted. I'm allowed to mourn the world I no longer have. I have to, in a way. To move forward into this new one.

* * *

There's no phone tag this time. Danny picks up. He doesn't recognize the number. I can tell by the way he says, "Hello?" The way he would pick up spam calls when we were dating. I told him to let them ring. Now I'm glad he doesn't.

"It's Ashley. Please don't hang up. I have something important to tell you."

This is not the ideal way to tell him. It's not even close. He likes texts. He likes to have time to process.

But we're going to be parents at eighteen. *Ideal* is not going to be possible. We'll do the best we can. That will have to be enough.

"I'm preg—"

"I know."

Wait, what? I fought so hard to work up the nerve. And he knew? How?

I hold back my questions. He needs time to think. And the next few minutes will shape the next few years. I know this.

"I found out when you got arrested. Jasleen was terrified. Madi told her everything. And when the two of them didn't hear anything after that, they decided to tell me. So I'd know why you were missing." He pauses. Like the next thing is costing a great effort. "They said you were planning to tell me. I . . . I get it."

I wait a second to make sure I heard right. To not say, "You do?" as if I'm shocked. I *am* shocked. Good shocked. "I'm sorry I didn't tell you sooner."

"You needed time. I wish I'd known, but I get it. That last fight was really messy. And to be totally honest, I didn't react this well when they told me." I hear what could be a gulp. Or it could be the lousy landline. "At least I got it out of my system before you called. Where are you? Are you okay? How are you doing?"

I remember last summer, how he'd ask me that when I came into the shop. *How are you doing?* And I'd say *fair to middling*, then complain about the heat. And our eyes would say we weren't talking about the weather.

That spark is gone forever. But this is the test of trust.

"Bad," I say. "Really bad. I did some incredibly stupid stuff. That you might think worse of me for."

"I heard. Remember, I found out from Jasleen and Madi after you got arrested. You don't have to—"

"Madi didn't know all of it," I say. "After I went to live with her, I was feeling so low. I took one of her pills again. Behind her back. You can tell her that. She must be feeling awful. After that, I got worried and told the doctor. And this happened. I'm so scared. I'm scared the courts will try to take Litt—I mean, our kid. When he's born."

Danny says, rock solid, "I won't let that happen."

It's a ridiculous thing to promise. But it makes me feel like our baby will be safe. Little Bean will have a father. In one way, at least, he'll have it better than I did.

"We need a lawyer," I say. Like we're a team.

"Jasleen has been calling everywhere. To find out who can help. She said the law is called Act 292 and it's been around for years. It lets them, uh, civil commit you. Basically in secret. To force you to get help if you're pregnant and they think you will use drugs."

"But I'm not getting help," I say. "I can't even take the vitamins that the baby needs. I haven't seen a doctor yet. This is supposed to be about helping? I reached out because I wanted help, and I ended up here instead. All it's done so far is make me want to die. The first night was brutal."

Danny's voice jumps. "Do you, uh, want to die right now? Are you safe where you are?"

I don't feel safe, but I don't feel suicidal either.

"I don't want to die anymore. I want to be free. They said they would give me a lawyer, but I haven't heard anything. I need to find one myself."

"About the lawyer. Maybe I can help. I, uh, mentioned this whole thing to a friend online. Without saying your name, of course. It's someone in *Elden Ring* fandom who's a paralegal. She works in a family law office, but she's not a lawyer. But she might know someone who can help. For cheap or free. What should I do if I get a name from her? Email you?"

I cannot get my hopes up. I cannot get my hopes up that Danny's gamer friend might just be able to help. I have to keep trying everything as if nothing has changed.

But it has. Whether this works or not.

"I don't have a computer here. I'm calling you from a landline. There's a different number for incoming. Write this down, okay? This is the number you can call."

He reads it back to me. Then Tasha comes up to say someone needs to call their social worker. Will I be done soon?

"I need to get off the phone," I say to Danny. "But thank you. For everything."

"No problem," Danny says. "Look, this is all weird and scary. Not what I expected. But I'm going to roll with it, okay? I'm going to fake it till I make it. And you hang in there. It's got to be scarier for you."

CHAPTER 23

If the past few months have taught me anything, it's this. Sometimes things you thought were fine spiral out of control. The world itself betrays you.

But also, sometimes what you thought was the scariest thing you could do . . . goes fine. The people who could have most let you down turn out to be the ones holding you up.

Sometimes the world is harsher than you expect. But the people by your side? They're better than you imagined.

I get calls every day. Cynthia's teasing but friendly "New girl, it's for you again!" is a joke shared across the floor. My mom checks in every day by phone. She visits twice a week. She's surprised I told Danny. She's even more surprised how well it went.

Danny calls regularly with updates. He's looking for a new job. Ice cream doesn't pay enough for a baby. He's thinking computer repair. He has practice with stuff like figuring out how to stop the graphics card on his desktop from overheating. It involves changing the hardware in some way I don't understand. But it sounds cool.

He passes on my hellos to Madi and Jasleen. He doesn't give them the number. I figure it looks better if I don't contact any of the Wendts yet. On account of how that's where I got the drugs. I have to think from the court's point of view. I hate it. But I'll do what I have to do for Little Bean.

Danny gives me all the news though. Including what Madi didn't want me to know. Yesterday, she told the police she'd shared her Xanax with me without telling me what it was first. She was convinced they'd take her prescription away. But they were confused by her trying to turn herself in. They let her off with a written warning.

It's wild to be stuck in this shelter without being charged with a crime. And here my friend who confesses to one is basically let go.

It's pretty obvious why. Rich people are allowed to be messy. They get second chances when the rest of us don't.

But I don't feel the way I sometimes do. I don't focus on the tension between how she cares about me and how her life is so different from mine.

Instead, I feel moved. She risked a lot for me. Including losing the medication that helped her when nothing else did. And this was after she found out that I snuck around behind her back the second time. She could have decided she owed me nothing after that.

And she doesn't owe me. Friendship isn't about debt. It's a choice to stick by each other and keep caring.

I don't know when I'll be able to talk to her again. But this kind of loyalty can stand the test.

Meanwhile, the hunt for a lawyer might be over. Jasleen worked her research miracles. And Danny's gamer contact came through for him. He gives me the names and phone numbers of both lawyers.

I keep telling myself not to get my hopes up. Legally, nothing is fixed yet.

But it's like the Emily Dickinson poem we had to write an essay on last year.

"Hope" is the thing with feathers -
That perches in the soul -
And sings the tune without the words -
And never stops - at all -

Hope rises in me. All broken-winged after the storm. It still flies up. Unstoppable. A creature of feathers and fire.

* * *

I ask the staffer on duty if I can use the phone to call a lawyer. Tasha is off today. Instead, it's the gruff woman who searched my bag that first night. She's less gruff when not dealing with unexpected arrivals. I still don't dare go over the ten-minute limit.

I decide to call Danny's online friend's recommended lawyer first. It feels too coincidental, too silly. A video game fan group can't possibly solve this.

Or maybe I'm embarrassed because I was kind of a jerk to Danny about his gaming. Back when we were dating.

No wonder he ended up flaking out on my dance stuff. It wasn't like I respected his big thing.

Now that Danny and I aren't trying to be a couple, I can appreciate him as a person more. I'm definitely not getting back together with him though. We don't need that kind of complication. Little Bean will need our shared focus. Not our shared mess.

By the amount of bloating I've had lately, Little Bean isn't so little anymore. Maybe I'll drop the first half of his name.

"Are you going to make that call, then?" The gruff staffer is back to check on me.

"Yes! Sorry. Sorry, I was just thinking." I start dialing as she stands over me. She leaves when the ringing starts, satisfied.

I look at the updated Firebird List. It's now a list of the facts I need a lawyer to know.

Ring, ring, ring.

"Hi, you've reached the legal office of Emilia Lambert."

At first, I think it's a voicemail. But when I wait for the tone, the secretary breaks her monotone.

"Hello?"

I start reading from the list.

"Hello. My name is Ashley Muller. I'm eighteen and pregnant. And I'm being detained under Act 292."

CHAPTER 24

Having a lawyer makes a difference. Emilia Lambert has seen at least fifty of these cases. She can tell me what to do. How to present myself. How to give the Bean and myself the best chance.

She's professional, but also kind.

"You matter too," she tells me. "Your baby is not the only one worth fighting for. You've been trying to be strong for him, but you deserve someone to defend *you*."

I try to believe that. The thought of being strong for someone else got me through the worst times. The times when I felt worthless.

But I'm not. *Flawed* is not the same as *worthless*. I repeat that to myself. A diamond can be flawed. Every person I love is flawed too. And yet they've rallied around me. They must all have those days too. When, in the depths of despair, only the thought of others who need them keeps them on their feet.

The day of the hearing, I think about how those who care about me have fought for me. And how I need to fight for myself.

* * *

Before I leave for court, Cynthia asks me if I want her email. To keep in touch once I'm out of here. Her next foster placement is coming soon. I trade contact info with her even though I'm not sure I'm getting out today. Hope seems worth it.

* * *

Once again, my hearing is the first in the morning. *In the interest of Baby Boy Muller*. Who is going to have the last name Morales. Or Hoffman. Whichever I want, according to Danny. And the other one for a middle name, I said. The last name should be Hoffman, he said. That might not be official till I change my own name. But Danny says that after all I've gone through, the baby should carry my name.

And the name of his grandmother, I think.

But he will not have the first name Francisco. Danny says it's too religious and not very unique. If I want a saint's name in Spanish, I should go for a weirder one.

I'm not sure unique or weird is what I'm looking for. Or a saint. Whatever.

Until we come up with something we both like, he's the Bean. The name reminds me how fragile everything is. How I'm planning for an uncertain future. But with human beings, that's the only kind of future you get.

* * *

It's Tasha who takes me to court. She's the one who's going to testify about my behavior. I'm relieved it's not the other staffer, the one who searched my stuff the first night.

When I walk into the courthouse, I'm fine. It's not until I go into the courtroom that it hits. Seeing the same three faces that undid me last time. I shrink.

This time I have someone on my side.

Emilia waves me over. Her goal is to present me as a responsible young woman who made a few bad decisions under the stress of losing the family home. Honestly, it sounds fake. Or at least, a fun-house mirror version of the truth.

I am a messier person than my lawyer says. And I want to set up some real counseling if I get out of here. I'll finally get something useful out of my health care plan. This winter proved I don't handle stress well. And life is not going to be less stressful with a baby.

But this hearing is not about truth. Neither was the last one.

What happened with the Xanax is not the main point. The point is how the court sees me. That will decide whether or not they let me go.

It's fake. It's unfair. It's a nasty way to figure out who's given back their freedom.

Emilia agreed with me when we talked about it earlier. Then she told me not to say that at the hearing.

"If I had my way, I'd get rid of this law," she said, shaking her head. "I don't think it helps. The fear and stress of being held by force . . . they make any treatment work less well. I don't think it's better for the baby. And even if it was?

I don't think it's worth what's being done to the person carrying the baby. Who's treated like a vessel."

I think about that last bit. At the first hearing, they didn't treat me like a vessel. Or an incubator. That's the way they talk about it in politics. But nobody hates an incubator the way they hate a pregnant teen.

Nobody thought of me as a thing. Everyone at the hearing thought of me as a person. A person who just wasn't worth it.

A baby is always "worth it." A baby is a fresh start. But when the baby is born, it becomes like everyone else. Almost as soon as it starts to breathe, it can be labeled. Poor. Disabled. The wrong color. All the labels people use against other people.

Every generation says they'll build a better world for their kids. It's a cliché. It doesn't happen. Sometimes they build a prison instead. Like my grandparents did for my mom.

Mom was raised Lutheran. She left their church because of how they treated her. After the divorce, she never took me back to church. She doesn't speak kindly of her Lutheran ancestors.

But when we learned about the Reformation in school, I thought of her. Not because of religion. Because when she walked away from her family and the husband they'd forced on her, she had come to the same place as Martin Luther when he stood up for his beliefs. After so long giving in to what others wanted, she broke away. She lived her own life. She found her own truth.

Here I stand. I cannot do otherwise.

And that must be why she's supported me through all this. Why she's let me make my own choices. Even when they aren't the ones she would have made.

Because everyone finds that choice in their lives eventually. The one they can't back down from. The one where they cannot do otherwise.

* * *

The commissioner comes in. The hearing begins.

CHAPTER 25

It's not that dramatic in the end. They let me go. They say I should be placed at home with my mother. I have to do drug tests and come back for another hearing in a month. That one will be called the final disposition.

I repeat the phrases my lawyer told me. *I deny the allegations in the petition. I reserve my right to request a jury.* I try to look respectable.

The commissioner says I seem steadier. More mature. That I benefitted from the month in the youth shelter. And that now that my mother's moved into the new apartment, I should be back with her. He trusts I'll come back for the final disposition hearing.

I try not to look skeptical. The main thing that's changed is I have someone to speak for me now. I keep my face still as he makes these claims.

The final disposition hearing is still ahead.

And I'm not free of child services yet. The threat of losing my baby still hangs over me. I won't feel safe till that's gone.

I thank Emilia for everything. She's going to stay on the case until it's all sorted out. Till the Bean is definitely staying with me.

Then Tasha drives me back to the youth shelter to pack up.

I'm going home. To a home I've never seen. It doesn't matter. I have a home to go to.

* * *

I put it all back in my backpack. The stuff I came in with. Cynthia's contact info. With "New Girl" written on top as a joke. Crossed out and replaced with "For Ashley."

And the Firebird List. I slide it in carefully. To remember how I got through this.

I never do get my razor or my deodorant back. I get to keep the new vitamins. Tasha makes sure of that. There's a moment of panic when the staff can't find my computer. Only my phone. They keep saying they never wanted to be responsible for electronics. But then they find it, just as my mom's car pulls up. I'm out the door without thinking. Finally free to leave without earning points. Out of my cage.

By the time we get to the new apartment, I'm worn out. It's been a long day. And I get tired more easily now.

Mom insists I open the mail. She collected it from Mr. Harrison in person. Which is enough of a sacrifice that I stop trying to escape to my new bedroom.

The envelopes are from the University of Wisconsin. I forgot the decisions were coming. It's like I sent the applications in another lifetime. It's hard to remember who I was when I wrote those essays. My body was different. My mind was different.

The mail from that past brings good news. I got into both the Madison and Milwaukee campuses. The Milwaukee aid package is bigger. I still miss the city I grew up in. What would it be like to go back as an adult?

But Madison has a program to help students with children pay for daycare. That could be huge for me.

I don't have to decide right now. I'll take some time to

consider what's best for the Bean. And also what's best for me.

I won't be able to put myself first anymore. Parents can't do that. The Bean will come first.

But I am also worth fighting for.

Mom hugs me like she'll never let go. I hug her back. Then I go crash in my room.

* * *

It's lucky I came home on a Friday. Two days to rest. To regain my strength. To start looking for a new doctor, and for some counseling. Then on day three, it's back to school. My secret is out. I'm not looking forward to going back.

But the group chat on my phone is encouraging.

Jasleen says I have nothing to be ashamed of.

Madi will blast anyone rude enough to comment with a stare of ice. Or liquid nitrogen, which is even colder.

Danny adds three fire emojis for agreement. He got the computer shop job and is starting a savings account for taking care of the Bean. But his new responsibilities don't stop him from cracking jokes in the group chat.

I try to have a sense of humor about my upcoming return to school too. *So the rumor mill will be facing both ice and fire*, I type, adding a *Game of Thrones* dragon GIF.

Then I put the phone down. Lie back on my familiar bed. Under a strange new ceiling. I touch the curve of my belly. *Hi there, Bean.*

I shut my eyes without pulling down the window shade. It's a still day. The sunlight makes fire dance behind my eyelids.

Things don't stay good forever. I'll forget how sweet this moment is. How bitter others were before. But if I keep the ups and downs I've survived in mind, maybe the dark times won't overwhelm me. I can steer my way through them instead of drifting. The rough, scary parts aren't over yet. They never really will be.

But I let myself feel this joy now. This freedom.

The way my heart has wings.

ABOUT THE AUTHOR

Maya Chhabra is the author of *Chiara in the Dark*, a YA novel-in-verse, and *Stranger on the Home Front,* a middle grade historical fiction novel. She has also written science fiction and fantasy short stories, and poetry based on myths and fairy tales. To learn more about her work as a writer and translator, visit mayachhabra.com. She lives in Brooklyn with her wife.